*meant*
for
*me*

# meant for me

**ERIN**
*New York Times* Bestselling Author
**MCCARTHY**

Cover © 2014 by Sarah Hansen, Okay Creations
Interior Designed and Formatted by

emtippettsbookdesigns.com

*more books by*
**ERIN McCARTHY**

**Blurred Lines Series**
*You Make Me*
*Live For Me*
*Let Me In*
*Meant for Me*
*Breathe Me In*


**The True Believers Series**
*True*
*Sweet*
*Believe*
*Shatter*


For a full list of over sixty books available visit:
www.erinmccarthy.net
www.facebook.com/ErinMcCarthyBooks

# *chapter* one

I WOKE UP THE WAY I always did after a drunken night- suddenly and with a feeling of panic. I had a mental checklist I always ran through when my eyes snapped open. First was to find my phone. I was in a darkened room buried under a giant purple comforter. Not my room. Not my much more masculine comforter. But habit usually had me tossing my phone on the nightstand even when I was loaded so that was always where I checked first. I felt around with a clumsy hand. Found it.

Next step was to make sure my wallet was with me. Fortunately, squinting as I rolled to the right, I saw it was next to my phone. I flipped it open. License and credit card still there. All good. I gave a shuddery sigh, my head giving the slow throb of a medium level hangover. Not the worst I'd ever had. Not the best. But I wasn't in imminent danger of throwing up, so I'd call it a win.

Third piece of information required was to figure out where
I was and who I'd had sex with, because I clearly wasn't at home
and this was no couch I was crashing on. It was a girl bed.
Everything was fluffy and pastel and smelled like patchouli. Plus,
I was naked, with both a partial erection and the sticky feeling
that my dick had been places it had no business being. Rolling
back carefully the other direction, both to avoid giving myself
dry heaves and to not wake up my new special friend, I studied
the girl who was sleeping with her mouth open.

Nope. I'd never seen her before in my life.

She was cute. At least even when shitfaced on Jager I had
good taste. Her cheekbones were long, her nose pert, her hair
long and blonde, though it was tangled to hell and back. A perfect
breast with a tight nipple was popping out of the blanket and I
wished I remembered actually having sex with this girl, because
most likely I'd enjoyed it. Which made the whole damn thing
totally pointless because I didn't. Not one single second of it was
coming back to me. The last thing I remembered was doing shots
with a girl who was definitely not this one. She'd been a brunette.

Sliding out of the bed, I moved as quietly as possible
gathering up my clothes. I was dressed, wallet back in my pants,
my phone in one hand, the other slowly turning the doorknob
when she woke up.

"Hey," she said sleepily. "Are you going to the bathroom?"

"I have to leave," I told her truthfully. "I'm going out of town
today." Also the truth. I was due to catch a ferry in a few hours
and I still had to drive to Rockland from Orono. After I showered
the stench of booze and sex off of myself. "I didn't want to wake

2

you up."

Her lip pulled down. "Really? You can't stay a little while?" She pushed the comforter down, revealing a perfect body, all curvy hips and tapered waist.

She was smooth everywhere and I found myself getting hard despite the dry mouth, despite the throbbing head, and despite the fact that I was due somewhere else by noon. Oh, and there was the little fact that I had no idea what her name was. But I hesitated. "I really have to go…"

She spread her legs a little and massaged her clitoris with her finger, pulling her lips open so I had a really pornographic shot of everything she had. "Oh, come on, Ethan. Please? I'm already ready, just come over here."

Way to make it easy for me. Damn. I adjusted myself in my jeans, making sure I'd be up to the task, because if I was, I was going back in. What difference did it make? She obviously had no regrets over the night before, so why should I? I didn't even have to finesse her or manage any foreplay, which I didn't think I was capable of at the moment. Plus she remembered my name, and deserved points for that.

"How could I resist that offer?" I said gruffly, yanking my shirt back off my head and pulling my jeans and boxers down just far enough to make it work as I climbed on top of her.

She groaned and dug her fingernails into my butt as I sank into her wet body. God, it felt so good. So bizarre that it did. That it could. I shoved the physical effects of drinking too much aside and isolated my focus to my cock, to the steady and soothing rhythm of me pumping into her over and over. I didn't kiss her, because of morning breath, and because well, that felt too intimate. This was fucking, nothing more, nothing less.

Her hips bucked up, grinding her clit against me, and she came with an arch of her back and a mewling cry that made me feel nothing. No satisfaction, no increased arousal. Nothing. I was masturbating with another human being. We both were. This was about me and the way her pussy made me feel hot and tight and ready to explode, and it was about her taking my dick and getting off on it. It wasn't about us. There was no us. It was totally selfish and greedy and because of that, I popped one off quicker than was courteous. But she'd got hers, so I could get mine and that was that.

I pulled out with a moan and kissed the tip of her nipple. "Good idea, thanks."

"Do you really have to leave?"

"Yep. I'm going to visit my sister. She just had a baby."

"Oh, tell Aubrey I said congrats."

"Sure." I would if I knew this girl's name. Clearly she knew my sister. I smacked the side of her hip, enjoying the sound flesh on flesh made. "You are fucking sexy, by the way. In case you didn't know." Standing up, I hiked up my jeans again.

She smiled and yawned. "Oh, I know." She laughed. "But thanks. Text me when you get back."

"Did you give me your number?" I checked to make sure my phone was still in the pocket of my pants.

She pulled a face. That pouting expression that proved I'd said something stupid and hurt her ego. Not her feelings, her ego. "Ethan, God, really? We were texting all night last night!"

There was no sugarcoating it. I shrugged. "And I was wasted. I don't remember half of what I did or said."

Now she really looked irritated. "You could at least pretend like you remember."

That made me curious. "Why? Why would that matter?"

"Because I don't want to hear that you only fucked me because you were drunk."

"I'm not drunk now and I just fucked you. Just because I don't remember that we texted doesn't mean I didn't want you then or now. I don't fuck girls I don't find attractive, even drunk." I was just attracted to a lot of girls lately. And they were all as equally willing as this one.

"You're an asshole." She pulled the comforter over her.

"I don't see why. I just told you I find you attractive." Moving towards the door, I paused, knowing I should let it go, but hungover enough to be cranky as hell. "Don't pretend you didn't know what you were doing. It's fun, that's all. There is no point in me lying to you and acting like we hooked up last night with anything else in mind."

"Just leave."

Fine. I could do that. "So am I supposed to text you or not? I need clarification."

Her answer was to hurl a pillow at me. It fell short of the mark. Knowing that I was being a dick even if I was just speaking the truth, I felt guilty and picked it up off the floor and placed it back on the foot of her bed. "Hey." I squeezed her foot beneath the blanket. "You're beautiful and I had fun. Let's do it again."

I didn't really want to see her again, but I felt compelled to lie to her. That's what she wanted, what all girls seemed to want. The lie, the illusion that we hadn't just had sex for the hell of having sex. They wanted to pretend it might mean something at some point, or at least that we were all so mature we could be friends with benefits instead of just strangers fucking in the dark.

But her blue eyes bore into me. "I don't think I want to see you again. They warned me about you, you know. That you're emotionally unavailable since Caitlyn, but I didn't believe them. Now I do."

My nostrils flared and I went still, hand still on her foot. Her words made me furious. No one had any right to toss Caitlyn at me when they didn't know me or jack shit about my relationship that had ended with her marrying someone else. It still hurt to think about Caitlyn and I knew I was going to be seeing her in the days to come since she lived down the road from Aubrey in Vinalhaven. I was already on edge. I didn't need this girl talking to me about my life, and the only girl I'd ever loved, like she knew a fucking thing.

"And how emotionally available am I supposed to be when we hooked up after a drunken night at the bar? Am I supposed to tell you my secrets? Fall in love with you? Grow up." It was harsh, I knew it was. But she had crossed a line and she was delusional if she thought we were supposed to mean anything to each other.

"Fuck you." Her lip quivered.

"I already did." Then feeling like the biggest asshole that there ever was, I left her room, pulling the door closed behind me. I had no idea where I was. It was a dorm, or a sorority house, though, definitely not an apartment building. The doors were too close together.

Feeling that I was too damn old to be screwing undergrads, I headed down the hall, and as I hit the top of the stairs I realized I was in my sister's old sorority house. Classy, Walsh. Half of the girls living there weren't even twenty-one. I had no idea if the girl I had just left was or not, and I felt the same disgust with myself I always did at some point after a night like I'd just had. I alternated between telling myself I didn't give a shit, and hating myself for my behavior. But it never stopped me. I did it over and over again, and I wasn't sure what addiction it was feeding, or how it was supposed to make me feel better.

All I knew was that I was no longer recognizable as the guy Caitlyn had been with. I had been a hard worker, thoughtful, kind, and I had loved Caitlyn with everything in me. I had felt like the luckiest guy in the world when I had proposed and she'd said yes and I'd had the whole future mapped out for us. Me in law school, her finishing her undergrad. A wedding, a house, good jobs, kids. And she'd left me without a glance for her high school boyfriend who as far as I could tell, had treated her like shit.

So maybe it had seemed the way to win with girls was to treat them like shit. But that was just me justifying. And I didn't want to win any of them anyway. I wanted to feel better short-term. I wanted attention. Sex. But I didn't want to date and I didn't want to open myself up to being hurt again.

Which meant I was stumbling down the stairs of the freaking sorority house in déjà vu for dickheads.

"Hey, Ethan," someone called out from the kitchen as I hit the bottom step.

Turning, I saw a girl I vaguely recognized and I raised my hand. "Hey."

These girls were all four to five years younger than me. What the hell was I doing? But it was hard to meet women my own age when I had dropped out of law school and I made a living tending bar. Of course I was meeting undergrads still in the party scene.

But law school was not an option for me at the moment. I'd been asked to take a leave of absence by my advisor before I failed out. After a semester of missing classes, showing up hungover, and bombing exams, it had been more than I expected, truthfully. They should have by all rights just booted my ass out, and I appreciated what he had been trying to do, but I wasn't even sure I wanted to go back. Which was ironic, since for the preceding decade of my life, that's all I had wanted- to be a lawyer. I didn't know what the hell I wanted now.

Whatever it was, I wasn't going to find it under the purple comforter of a girl I barely knew. Sober I knew that. Drunk it didn't seem to matter much. I wasn't looking for anything or anyone so much as it was finding me.

Shoving open the front door I stepped out onto the sidewalk and winced as the bright light of mid-morning hit my eyes. I desperately wanted sunglasses and an iced tea the size of my head but neither was to be had at the moment. Setting out on foot, I wondered how Blond Girl and I had gotten back to the sorority house. Presumably we'd walked. I hoped like hell we'd walked. Glancing through my phone, I found a whole mess of text messages from someone named Lila. Scrolling to see what we'd written, I found it was a bunch of nonsense and drunken sexting. But there was also a picture of her showing me her tits. Blond Girl=Lila. One mystery solved. Never in a thousand years would I have guessed that was her name.

It was hot outside and my balls were sticky. The day was

not starting off in a promising way. I also had a text from my sister reminding me what time the ferry was. Annoyed that she thought I needed some kind of hand-holding, I texted back a short response.

*Got it.*

What, like Aubrey had any right to jump my shit? She had stayed with a complete douchebag for over a year, and while no one else was willing to say anything, I could do math. There was no way in hell her baby was her new husband's kid unless Emma had been born a month premature. Since she was born at eight pounds and change, I was guessing she'd been right on time and the abusive prick Jared was actually Emma's biological father. I wasn't going to say anything though. If they wanted to keep a secret and keep Jared from having any say in Emma's life, I was down with that. It seemed smarter and safer long term.

But I didn't need Aubrey judging me. Not when our whole lives she'd been the loose screw and I was the poster child for responsibility. I was going through a rough patch. Deal with it.

Of course I realized immediately when she responded that she hadn't been judging me at all. That was me putting my shit- my guilt- onto her.

*Yay! So excited to see you.*

I was a defensive dick. Truth.

I sent her a smiley face. *Me too.*

I was. I'd be even more so if she wasn't living in the same airspace as Caitlyn and Heath.

It pissed me off that two years later I still wasn't over Caitlyn. Like what the hell? I should have moved on a long ass time ago. I wasn't even sure why it still bothered me so much. Did I still love her?

I didn't know. Not exactly. She was a stranger to me now.

But there were times, like when I buried myself in a girl like Lila, whose come on wasn't even remotely subtle, and who could have substituted me for a dozen different guys, when I remembered what it had felt like to be with Caitlyn. How I had spent hours stroking her hair, her face, her lips, her skin. How I'd looked at her and everything in my chest had swelled. How I had loved coaxing her desire to life, watching her eyes widen in understanding of pleasure as I touched her, and I missed that intimacy so bad it hurt in every goddamn inch of me.

It wasn't about Caitlyn's lack of sexual experience or the fact that girls like Lila were comfortable in their own skin and hadn't lacked for partners. I didn't care what anyone did in her sex life and I didn't judge casual sex. I just knew it was destroying me at the same time I didn't seem to be able to resist it. Because what I missed was that tenderness, that connection that fused the physical and the emotional because you really dug someone. I had loved Caitlyn and she had cared about me. I knew that. Maybe it hadn't been forever love for her, but she would have married me if Heath hadn't shown up out of nowhere.

So I guessed I owed him one for showing up sooner than later. How much worse would it have been later, after marriage, kids? A lot worse. An avalanche instead of a few rocks falling.

Now there was a comfort. Jesus.

When I got back to my apartment I stripped off my clothes in the bathroom and let them fall to the floor. After turning on the shower I leaned against the counter and texted Lila.

*I'm sorry, that was rude.*

Whatever she needed or wanted to tell herself I had no right to be an asshole to her. If I was going to play the game, I had to stick to the rules. And the rules were you pretended you weren't just two random strangers getting each other off.

*Whatever.*

That was her response. But I knew that wouldn't be the end of it. She wouldn't be able to let it rest at that. By the time I'd gotten into the shower, washed my hair and body and stood under the spray letting it massage the knots out of my shoulders, and then climbed back out, dripping wet, she'd already texted again.

*When do you get back?*

*Tuesday.*

*Let me know if you want to hang out.*

*K. I definitely do.*

Did I? I really didn't know. I couldn't remember a single word of conversation we'd had the night before. But it was the right thing to do, or so it seemed. It was polite or something, which was just stupid. Why did it matter?

But it still did.

As I walked into my kitchen with a towel around my waist, my hair sticking up damp in all directions from where I'd scrubbed it with the towel, my phone buzzed again.

*I do too. I had a lot of fun talking to you, you make me laugh.*

Then as if she'd immediately realized that was too emotional, too revealing, her next text was sexual. It was like a default setting we all chose when we were getting uncomfortable.

*And you make me come too. Haha.*

*Good. I can make you come again.*

*I know you can.*

I grabbed a soft drink out of the refrigerator and opened it. I drank half of it in one gulp.

When I apparently didn't answer Lila fast enough, she texted again.

*You like anal? I bet you could talk me into it.*

Suddenly I felt my stomach turn and it wasn't from the cold carbonation hitting my gut after all the alcohol. It was because this girl, who was beautiful and most likely intelligent, thought she needed to dangle sexual carrots in front of me to hold my interest. And she was right. And that meant neither one of us had any business spending one fucking minute in each other's company.

*We'll see. I'm jumping in the car now to drive to my sister's ttyl. Have a good weekend.*

That was as much as I could deal with Lila and the supposedly uncomplicated aspect of a hook up that was in fact totally complicated, soul sucking, and basically never worth it. For a few minutes of pleasure I got baggage, guilt, expectation. It was more than I could handle on a Saturday when I had to drive to Rockland and meet my baby niece. And see Caitlyn.

Getting dressed I was almost glad I was finally going to see her again. It had been so long and I had thought about it so much, it was like this meeting had become the monster I was hiding from for so long I'd forgotten why it was scary. It couldn't possibly be as horrible as I had built it up to be.

Yet for whatever reason, after I got dressed, I opened my top dresser drawer and pulled out the ring box that was sitting in there behind my underwear. Flicking open the lid, I saw the diamond engagement ring that I had spitefully asked Caitlyn to return to me when we broke up.

Snapping the box shut again, I shoved it into the pocket of my shorts, grabbed my keys, and left the apartment.

# *chapter*
# two

$B$Y THE TIME I GOT to Rockland and boarded the ferry, my headache had receded but I was tired and hungry. The breeze was great though, and I sank down onto a bench out in the open air, grateful to close my eyes against the sun and relax a bit before being inundated with Aubrey's enthusiasm. She had texted me a half dozen times in the last two hours. There were a couple of kids running around the ferry and I watched them, feeling pissed off at myself and annoyed at the world in general.

It was just the post-alcohol crash. That high of the night before followed by the inevitable physical weariness and the thoughts of what the hell was I doing with my life? I wanted to stretch out full length on the bench and take a nap for the hour long ferry trip but a girl had sat down at the end of my row. Glancing over at her, I wondered how rude it would be to stand up and move to another bench so I could lie down. But this was the only one in full sun and when I looked at her, I accidentally caught her eye.

She gave me a tentative smile, her dark hair falling forward to cover her cheek when she tucked her head in a shy gesture that disarmed me. When was the last time a woman had looked at me like that? A long time. Years. Without thought, I smiled back.

"Hi," I said, because well, it was polite.

She smiled again, but didn't say anything.

"Do you care if I lie down?" I asked. "I'd like to take a nap." There was enough room for me to stretch out and still not touch her, but my feet would be fairly close to her. Hopefully she wouldn't care, because I needed twenty minutes with my eyes closed or I was going to be passing out in my dinner at Aubrey's.

Her light blue eyes widened but she didn't say anything. She just shook her head to indicate she didn't object.

"Thanks." Sticking my sweatshirt behind me on the plastic armrest at the end of the bench, I pulled my legs up and settled back. It actually gave me a direct view of her. She was in her late teens, fair skin, a narrow, exotic face, with plump lips. Dressed in denim shorts and a billowy white shirt. I could see she was long and lean. She played with her hair repeatedly, making sure she was never looking at me. Definitely beautiful, but definitely not my type.

As in, she wasn't drunk and flirting outrageously with me on first glance.

The ferryboat operator came over to her and waved. "Hi, Chloe. How is your dad?"

She smiled up at him but she didn't answer. She just nodded.

"Do you think you'd be free to babysit sometime soon? The wife and I could use a night out without the kid."

She nodded again.

"Friday?"

That got a thumb's up from her.

What the fuck? Didn't this chick talk?

The ferryboat operator didn't look like he thought it was weird at all. He just smiled down at her. "Great. The wife will text you." He squeezed her shoulder as he moved away. "Tell your dad I'll ring him up about getting some lobster."

Another nod.

Squinting, I didn't even pretend to look away when she turned and realized I had been watching the entire exchange. Her cheeks tinted pink, but she didn't look away.

"So you live on Vinalhaven?" I asked.

Nod.

"Maybe you know my sister then. Aubrey Walsh. Well, Aubrey Riker now."

Another nod.

Quite the conversationalist. Not. I tried again. "Your name is Chloe?"

Nod.

"I'm Ethan."

She gave me a little wave. For acknowledgement I guessed.

So she wasn't going to talk. That was obvious. Weird. Was she a nun in training? A cult member? Deaf? It didn't seem like she was reading lips, nor did she seem to have any trouble understanding what me or the other guy had said. She just was… silent.

Okay then. Islanders were a unique bunch. Clearly this girl fit right in. "I'm going to visit Aubrey," I said, which was stupid and obvious. "Do you know how I get to her house?"

Her lips pursed and her brow knitted together. She put her palms flat on her knees then she raised them and dropped them again. Then pointed to the right.

"Uh…" Then suddenly I realized what she was doing. "I go right off the ferry?"

She nodded, a small shy smile replacing the concentrated look.

"Thanks." So she really was speech impaired in some way or she would have just said something. I felt like an ass for pestering her with questions. I gave another smile then tucked my hands behind my head and closed my eyes so she wouldn't feel self-conscious with me looking right at her. Plus I really did want a nap. The sun was hot, but I felt like I was baking the alcohol out of me and it was a satisfying sensation.

I fell asleep and only woke up when the boat bumped against the dock in Vinalhaven. My waking was more leisurely than it had been at Lila's. I wasn't worried about where I was or what I might have lost. Instead I pried my eyes open slowly and stretched. The girl, Chloe, was no longer on the bench with me. After a minute, I forced myself to sit up and cracked my neck. I was feeling a lot better and I was finally hungry. I hoped Aubrey's new found domestic talents included cooking. I wanted food. Playing with my phone, I discovered that my GPS couldn't seem to figure out where the hell I was. I had assumed I could just enter Aubrey's address into my phone and get directions. You know, like everywhere else in America. But no, my phone seemed thoroughly confused as to what was happening.

I texted my sister.

*How do I get to your house?*

*Walk up the road out of town. Turn right.*

Helpful. In a very vague and nebulous way.

But I'd figure it out.

Putting my phone back in my pocket, I exited the ferry with the dozen or so other passengers. When I wound up in the parking lot, I saw Chloe was standing there waving. I wasn't sure she was waving at me so I glanced behind me but there was no one there. I waved back, figuring if she wasn't then whatever. It wasn't like I was ever going to see her again. But she approached me and shoved her cell phone at me. Startled I took it, glancing at the screen. She had the notes app up and on it was written, "I live next door to Aubrey. Follow me."

"Oh," I said out loud. "Cool. Thanks." I handed her the phone back, still curious as to what the absence of speech was all about.

Also, how did you make casual conversation with a chick who didn't talk? I could just hear my frat brothers making cracks about how that would be the best possible woman to hang out with- one who didn't talk. But the reality was it was awkward as she started across the parking lot and I fell into step beside her. I could see now that she was standing right next to me that she wasn't quite as young as I'd first thought. She was just lithe and delicate but definitely out of high school.

She was typing on her phone. After a minute she showed it to me. *You look like Aubrey.*

I smiled. "No, Aubrey looks like me. I'm older. I got first pick of the gene pool."

She didn't say anything.

And then I realized that was a completely inane thought to have. Of course she didn't say anything. She was obviously never going to say anything. "Do you have any siblings?"

Her brow wrinkled again in displeasure and I wondered why that seemed to be the wrong thing to ask. She raised her index finger to indicate one and then looked away, back at the water.

Two year earlier, I would have kept trying to communicate with her, put her at ease. But she had looked away, and I was hungry, and the last two years had eroded some of my charm and manners. I figured let her get my attention if she wanted to have a pseudo conversation. Caitlyn's ring kept shifting in my pocket and I regretted bringing it. Pausing for a minute, I dropped my backpack to the ground and took the box out of my pocket. I shoved it in the side pocket and tossed it over my shoulder again. Chloe was watching me. Her blue eyes were curious and intelligent. Expressive.

I felt like she knew what had been in the box, that she knew it was Caitlyn's ring. That she knew I was a fucking mess and she judged me for it. I felt flustered suddenly, realizing how damn ridiculous that was. She couldn't know anything about me. She was just waiting for me, and yes, she was probably curious. Who wouldn't be?

"Do you ever wonder why the hell you do something?" I asked rhetorically. "I don't know why I brought that with me."

She nodded. I could see in her blue eyes that she understood what I was getting at. It was bizarre to me that she could effectively communicate without words. Maybe in a way it removed the white noise of verbal clutter. Maybe sometimes we talked too much or around the subject. Chloe just nodded or shook her head. Agree or disagree. Nothing more. No running dialogue or theory. Yet at the same time, it was frustrating in its simplicity. What was the thought passing through her head? It made me curious.

"I was engaged to Caitlyn Deprey," I said, conversationally. Why, I wasn't sure. I never talked about Caitlyn. But there was something easy about confiding in someone who seemed empathetic but would have zero opinion to offer. "That's the ring I was going to give her. I asked for it back, which was really shitty of me. And all I've done with it is let it sit in a drawer. I almost feel like I should give it back to her so she can sell it. I mean, it was a gift. You shouldn't ask for a gift back, right? I did it because I was pissed off."

Chloe was biting her lip, the soft fabric of her shirt shifting at the hem in the breeze as she glanced over at me. Then she started typing on her phone. After a second, she showed me the screen.

Squinting in the sun, I read it.

How long ago did you break up?

"A stupidly long time ago."

She typed again. Maybe it doesn't matter now?

I gave a snort. "Ha. Good point." The only one it mattered to was me. I was the loser who hadn't moved on. Way to feel pathetic at two in the afternoon. "I guess it doesn't matter at all."

Swallowing hard, I stared out at the water. Vinalhaven was exactly like I'd imagined it- clapboard buildings dropped here and there with no plan or order, the harbor dotted with boats, both fishing and sailboats. It had the briny scent of the ocean clinging to it, and commercial and residential dwellings interspersed along the coastline. We were going right. Apparently that was all I needed to know. Go right and you'll get there. If only life were that fucking simple. Now I had no clue which direction to take. A small hand on my arm jerked me out of my dark and cyclical thoughts.

Startled, I turned to see Chloe staring at me.

"I'm sorry," she mouthed.

There was something beautiful about her silent sympathy. That she didn't know me at all, but felt compelled to try to tell me she felt bad. She was compassionate, that was obvious. Yet at the same time that my chest swelled and I felt the stirring of gratitude, I hated that she would see me like this. That somehow I had become a victim. A victim. Like the kind of guy other dudes made fun of and girls felt sorry for because I had lost. I had lost the girl to another guy and I had lost in the aftermath because I had done nothing to prove that I had ever been worthy of her in the first place.

Staring at Chloe made me hate myself. In her face, I saw reflected back at me every poor choice I'd made, every girl I'd fucked, every day that stretched ahead of me with zero purpose whatsoever. It was on the tip of my tongue to tell her I didn't want her goddamn sympathy, but I stopped myself. I couldn't do that to her. It had nothing to do with her and for whatever reason she didn't talk, I couldn't spit in the face of her fairly bold gesture of attempting to communicate with me.

"Thank you," I said, my voice raw and low. "It's okay, you know." Maybe it wasn't okay. I didn't know. I wasn't even sure why it mattered so much. Like who the hell hadn't been hurt in a relationship? Everyone who had ever breathed, basically. So why was this such a big deal to me?

No answers. I'd spent a long time looking for them and they weren't showing up. Maybe they never would. That was a pleasant thought. Chloe's hair had fallen into her eyes and without thinking about it, I reached out and brushed it off her cheek. She sucked in her breath and pulled back. I realized that it wasn't appropriate to touch a stranger that intimately. Not really. But I did it all the time. Every time I went out I touched someone in a way that was personal, suggestive, intimate. It had warped my sense of what was okay and why we touched someone in the first place.

I dropped my hand. "Sorry. I didn't mean to freak you out. You just had a hair in your eye."

She didn't say anything.

Jesus. I suddenly wanted to get the hell away from her. It was too bizarre and more than I could handle before I'd eaten anything for the day. She made me think too hard and it was uncomfortable.

We walked up the road and left the vestiges of town behind in that businesses disappeared and only houses were strewn about here and there. When we had gone another twenty minutes in silence and I was sweating bullets in the summer sun, wishing a beer would magically appear in my hand, she finally paused in front of a house that might have been painted gray or maybe was just weathered to the point that the boards appeared gray. She pointed to the house and then to her chest.

"That's your house?"

She nodded.

"Okay, thanks for getting me this far, I really appreciate it."

She stretched her arm out and pointed to the next house down the road, then to me.

"Aubrey's?"

Nod.

"It was nice to meet you, Chloe. Maybe I'll see you around town."

She nodded with a quick smile and started up the driveway.

For the first time, it occurred to me to wonder what she had been doing on the ferry. Who let a girl who didn't speak go to the mainland by herself? What had she been doing there? It was a mystery. One I wasn't sure I cared enough to solve.

I didn't seem to care about much besides avoiding reality and making myself feel like shit repeatedly.

# *chapter*
# three

UBREY'S HOUSE WAS ABOUT AS weatherbeaten as Chloe's and even smaller. It was tired, with no bushes or landscaping besides one lone pot of flowers sitting on the edge of the porch. It didn't look like a place my sister would want to hang out. It had a barn, for fuck's sake. Aubrey was a suburban girl. She was Abercrombie and Fitch. She was jaded and complaining.

But then again, maybe that was just my perspective as her older brother. I hadn't spent much time with her in the last year. Hell, even before that. From everything she had said, she was happy here. Maybe she'd been a bit of a whiner before because she hadn't found her place.

She'd figured out where she belonged and I had lost any sense of what to do with my life. Total role reversal. Not a comfortable feeling.

Going up onto the sagging porch, I knocked on the door. She answered immediately, the door swinging open and revealing her standing there in athletic shorts and a tank top, her chest bursting out of it like the shirt no longer fit. Her hair was no longer blonde, but a reddish tone, and she was smiling widely. But the biggest change was that in her left arm was a chubby baby facing out towards me, bubbles forming on her lips.

Whoa. My sister was a mother. Seeing it made it definitely one hundred percent real.

"Hi!" She reached out and gave me a one-arm hug, partially squishing the baby between us.

Aubrey looked and sounded so cheerful it made me feel totally melancholy and I wasn't even sure why. I was happy for her. I'd missed her. "Hey. So what have we got here?" I bent over and checked out the baby, running my finger over her cheek. Her skin was softer than I would have guessed. I hadn't spent much time around babies and the way she stared up at me, solemn, her brown eyes glassy, her features all in miniature perfection, kind of blew me away.

My sister bounced the baby a little in her cradle hold. "This is Emma. Say hi to your Uncle Ethan, Emma."

Then she did the unthinkable and tried to hand the baby to me. "I don't think…" But then I was holding her, awkwardly for a second, then settling into it, and my protests died. She smelled like skin and diapers and something else I couldn't place. Her head lolled a little and I shifted her so that I could hold her safely and check out her little face. She was pretty damn cute, there was no denying it. "Hey, Emma. Look at you with your perfect little nose, and your tiny little lips."

Aubrey laughed.

God, I heard myself and had to laugh too. I sounded like every other idiot talking nonsense to a baby.

"Come on in," she said, moving into the house. "I'm so glad you're here. I wish you could meet Riker but there's plenty of time for that. He'll be back in six weeks. You'll have to come up again."

Carefully walking with Emma in my arms, I followed Aubrey, glancing around curiously. The inside of the house wasn't as worn as the outside. It was small but clean. "You guys own this house?"

"No, we rent it. But I like it okay. It's not too big, not too small. The kitchen is retro, but whatever." She sank down onto the couch. "I'm not working so this is perfect for a one income family."

So adult. That was what struck me about her. Aubrey looked calm, happy. She had a family of her own. She wasn't just a daughter and a sibling any more. She was a wife. A mother. Freaky shit for a big brother to realize that his little sister was all grown up and then some. Maybe it wouldn't seem so real if I had one ounce of my own shit together. But I didn't.

"You look great," I told her, and I meant that. She looked beautiful in her peacefulness. I sat down in the easy chair carefully, descending with the baby in my arms. Emma made a face like she was going to cry and I felt a momentary panic. "Crap, I think she's going to cry. What do I do?"

"Bounce her a little."

I attempted a bounce. The baby let out a protest, making the first actual sound since I'd arrived.

Aubrey laughed. "Maybe I should have said gently rock her. You just bounced her like a basketball."

Emma started crying for real now, louder than I could have ever imagined a human being that tiny could manage. Her face was all screwed up and red, and a fat wet tear rolled down her cheek. That was it. I was out. Standing up, I foisted the baby back at Aubrey. "You'd better take her."

She rolled her eyes at me. That looked more like my sister.

"Ethan, I don't think I've ever seen you look so scared in your life."

"Lack of experience, what can I say? I feel like I made her cry."

"You didn't make her cry. She's hungry. See how her lips are trying to suck on nothing?"

I eyed the baby. "Yeah, I guess."

Suddenly Aubrey pulled her tank top and did something to her bra and then her breast was just there, nipple and all, for a split second before the baby blocked it. "What the fuck are you doing?" I asked, horrified.

"I'm feeding my baby." Another eye roll.

I looked at the floor. "I get that but holy shit, give me some warning so I can look away."

"It's not like you haven't seen about a thousand boobs in your lifetime."

Possibly a slight exaggeration. "You're my sister. The creepy factor is high, I'm sorry." Really high. Like so high I needed to distract myself in an attempt to banish that visual from my memory banks. "So, uh, what's with your neighbor?"

"Paul? What about him?"

"Not Paul. Chloe. The girl who doesn't talk. I met her on the ferry. What's the story there?" Glancing up, I saw Aubrey had adjusted her shirt so she was covered, Emma blocking the rest of her. But nonetheless I concentrated on my sister's face as I spoke.

"What do you mean? Chloe is Paul's daughter."

"Why doesn't she talk?" I asked impatiently. That wasn't a normal thing. There was a reason for it.

"She has selective mutism. It's caused by anxiety. I guess she's been like that since she was seven."

What the hell? Astonished, I asked, "She hasn't talked since she was *seven*?"

"Well, she talks to her father though I've never seen it, and she will occasionally whisper in her little sister's ear. I have seen her do that."

Okay, that just totally threw me. "Wait a minute. So you mean she can talk, she just doesn't? Like she's mute on purpose, for a dozen years? Who does that?"

My God, no one in my family could go twenty minutes without saying something. A decade of silence? It was crazy.

"It's not on purpose," she said, and there was censure in her voice. "From what I understand, she wants to talk, she just can't in front of anyone she isn't totally comfortable with."

"That's weird," I said flatly. "She's pretty enough. I don't get it."

"What does that have to do with anything?"

"I don't know. It just seems if you're bullied or socially anxious or whatever it's because you have something about you that makes you an easy target, like a disability or a physical deformity. I mean, it's terrible to say, but true. Usually being pretty guarantees a reasonable amount of social success."

"You sound like an asshole," she said.

"What?" I protested. "It's true. I just think it's odd and really pretty damn sad that this girl doesn't talk when she probably hasn't been brutalized or bullied like some kids."

"You're quantifying her pain?"

That made me pause. "No. Yes. I don't know. Has she gotten treatment?" The conversation was starting to make me uncomfortable and I wasn't sure why exactly. Maybe because I was sitting from that place of privilege I was ascribing to Chloe. I always had been. Good parents, suburban upper middle class upbringing, an overachiever. Well liked by my classmates. Aubrey was right to be looking at me like that. But it still seemed bizarre as hell. I was standing by that.

"I don't know. She's my neighbor and my babysitter but I've never asked her. Like how would I say that? Hey, are you trying to fix your shit? It's rude." Aubrey lifted Emma up to her shoulder and pulled her shirt down. As she rubbed Emma's back, she narrowed her eyes. "Why are you so interested anyway?"

I shrugged. "It's not every day you meet someone who doesn't speak. In fact, this is a first for me. I find it strange that you aren't more interested. And did you say she's your babysitter?"

"Yes. She's great with Emma. I asked her to come over tonight so we can go into town and get some pizza. I didn't have time to go to the grocery store and buy food."

That shattered my dreams of being well fed. Domesticity didn't extend to cooking apparently. But I had to ask. "Do you really think it's a good idea to leave your two month old with a girl who doesn't talk?"

"Why does she need to talk? Emma doesn't talk either." She was looking at me like I was a moron.

"Because she can't call 911 if something happens."

"She's mute, not stupid."

Frustrated, I ran my fingers through my hair and shook my hair. "Alright, got it. Mind my own damn business."

"I'm not saying you have to mind your own business. I just don't get it. If she dials 911 they'll show up here. What is the big deal?"

"I don't know. Never mind." Bottom line was, I wasn't a parent. If she didn't think it was an issue, I needed to shut the fuck up. I didn't know a damn thing about taking care of a baby.

"How are you?" she asked.

Immediately her words made me feel defensive. "What do you mean?" That was a 'bless your heart,' tone of voice.

"I mean, how are you? You dropped out of law school. Mom says you're drinking a lot." She made a face. "I mean, I don't know what Mom's definition of a lot is. Maybe you have two beers on Friday. But I'm asking you- how are you?"

"I'm fine." I raised my eyebrows up and down. "Though I could use a beer right now. And that pizza. What time did you want to go because I'm starving."

"Smooth. But don't think I'm just going to forget what we were talking about because you changed the subject. I may have baby brain right now, but I haven't totally lost my edge."

I snorted. "What edge? You're not a card shark."

"I have an edge!" She laughed.

Emma gave a rip roaring burp, her head wobbling backwards.

"Damn. Your baby sounds like you."

Aubrey stuck her tongue out at me. "Jerk."

"Brat."

Yeah, this was our sibling relationship exactly as it always had been. It was actually reassuring. There were certain things in life that should never change.

"So can you believe the difference a year makes?" Aubrey asked. "God, when I got here last year, I was messed up from Jared, thinking a place like this was good for hiding, nothing more. And now I can honestly say I expect to live here forever, raising Emma and another baby or two with Riker."

Aubrey had a brightness, a glow, a pink-cheeked, glassy-eyed good health and happiness thing going on that made me feel both tremendously grateful she'd found her place, and melancholy as hell. "That is nuts. And a year ago, I thought I had my shit together." I raised my eyebrows up and down to indicate it was a joke, that I didn't particularly care. "Can I hold Emma again? Is she done eating? And by the way, how do you know a baby is done eating?"

"You know she's done because she either falls asleep, or she stops sucking, or she pulls back and milk is dribbling off the corner of her mouth."

"And I'm sorry I asked." When I'd gotten engaged to Caitlyn, I'd actually thought I was ready to get married and start a family oh, about now. Yeah. Totally not ready.

Then again, maybe if I was in love, and in a healthy relationship, I would be. Emma was pretty damn cute. I stood up and reached for the baby. Aubrey lifted her up to me a la Simba in *The Lion King* and I clumsily put my hands under her warm body. "Don't let go until I'm sure I have her." The thought of dropping my niece and giving her brain damage seemed like the worst possible exclamation point to my year of fucking up. "Okay, got her."

Aubrey looked bemused. I found it interesting that she wasn't a neurotic new mother, making me wash my hands and take a first aid course before touching Emma.

"She looks like Dad, don't you think?"

"God, I hope not." My father was a decent looking guy, hell, I looked like him, but Emma was a girl. She didn't need balding in her future. "Then again, she doesn't have much more hair than he does."

She laughed. "Well, considering Dad has been way cooler about all of this than Mom, I think it's only fair."

"Mom is a control freak." It was a family trait. Running my hand over Emma's wispy blonde hair, I marveled at how adorable she was, and how serious her expression was. "She's very intense. Emma, I mean."

"I think she's like her uncle that way. So what happened with law school, Ethan? For real. You know I won't say anything to Mom and Dad."

I looked up at my sister. "It's no mystery and it's no secret. I partied too hard and I was doing lousy so I withdrew before they kicked me out."

"But why were you partying? Why *are* you partying?"

She wasn't going to let me get away with the obvious, apparently. "I don't know. Not exactly. I mean, the breakup with Caitlyn screwed me up. Then I started throwing over all my rules, you know? About drinking and hookups and what motivates me to get through the day. And it occurred to me that if I could do all that, then I wasn't really sure about anything."

It also occurred to me that I kept thinking of my breakup with Caitlyn as being not that long ago, but it would be two years in a couple of months. Damn. Chloe was right. It didn't matter anymore.

"Ethan." Aubrey's expression had softened. It was sympathy, but it was more than that- it was understanding. "I know what it's like to just be on a ride that you don't really like and you have no idea how to exit. But the thing is at some point you have to just jump off it, you know what I'm saying? You'll be glad you did."

I could see her point. "But what if I break a few bones when I jump? On the ride I know what I'm getting."

"Yeah. Nauseous."

I laughed. "Good point."

There was a knock on the door. "That's probably Chloe," she said.

Emma was doing that burbling thing again. Her mouth was like a chemistry beaker- it just kept oozing. When did babies learn to contain their own spit, I wondered. I pondered that and tried not to be curious when Chloe came into the room. I was even more weirded out now that I knew she was mute by choice. Or not exactly by choice, as Aubrey had instructed me, but because of a disorder that presumably could be fixed. It wasn't a physical limitation.

Chloe waved to me, a shy smile playing about her lips.

She really was a beautiful girl. With very little makeup she would look glamorous, even girl-next-door fresh. Maybe it was a good thing she was on this rock of an island, protected from men who would prey on her and her disability.

"Hi, Chloe," I said. "Thanks for babysitting." Standing up, I walked over so I could pass the baby to her.

She nodded.

# *meant* for *me*

Aubrey was talking about diapers and where the bottles where and mom crap, but I didn't think Chloe was listening to her. She was watching me carefully under her eyelashes, and I could see the rapid rise and fall of her chest as I invaded her space. For the sole purpose of giving her the baby, of course. I couldn't go there. Wouldn't go there. You couldn't hand a baby over from five feet away though. Our hands touched and I heard Chloe's breath suck in. She was looking at Emma now, not me, but I could feel her nervousness.

Suddenly, that was the last thing I wanted. I didn't want her to feel I was a predator. That I wanted something from her. That she was an object to entertain me. "Got her?" I asked gruffly.

She nodded.

I stepped away. "Thanks. Aubrey, I'm sorry, can you repeat all of that? I accidentally distracted Chloe."

Aubrey gave me a curious look but she started to repeat her instructions, moving closer to Chloe. I drifted towards the door. I had distracted Chloe without meaning to. That was it. Nothing more. Nothing less.

Emma cried and Chloe shifted her to her shoulder, gently rocking her back and forth and making shushing noises. It was the first sound I'd heard from Chloe's lips and it seemed strange that she could do that and yet couldn't force words out. But a baby was a forgiving audience.

As soon as she realized I was watching her, she stopped.

It made me feel even more worthless than I had when I had woken up that morning in Lila's bed.

For the first time in a very long ass time, I wanted something different. Something better.

# *chapter* four

AS I ATE AN ENTIRE pizza solo, and Aubrey picked her way through two slices, we talked about being kids, having kids, Riker, and the probability that our father was a closet alcoholic. The usual. It was easy and casual and comfortable.

Until she brought up Caitlyn. "She and Heath are planning to get married next summer."

I dropped my final piece of pizza down half eaten and took a swallow of my beer. "I guess that's not surprising. They've been together awhile now."

"You don't have to see her while you're here, you know. She got a job teaching, and Heath is out on his boat every day. And it's not like I was planning to invite them over for happy hour or anything."

Reflecting on my feelings, I said, "I think I need to see her.

Maybe it's the way I can finally let go. Because I'm blaming her for changing my life and that's not fucking fair. I know it's not. She had to do what she had to do, what was right for her."

"You actually broke up with her," Aubrey reminded me. "She didn't get back with Heath until you ended things."

"That's a technicality and you know it." I didn't really want to rehash this. "She wanted to be with him, she was just trying to hedge her bets by staying with me."

"You don't know that. I think she was genuinely torn between the two of you."

"Fine." I was done with the conversation. "It's time to put that chapter of my life behind me. It's long overdue. She clearly has." The idea of her getting married wasn't particularly upsetting. It had been my assumption they would at some point. Frankly, I'd been surprised they hadn't already. "I'll text her and see if I can stop by and say hi."

"With Heath there?" Aubrey shook her head. "Just let me invite her over and then you can be there."

That didn't seem any less obvious to me, but if that's what Aubrey thought was best, I wasn't really sure I cared one way or the other. "Sure."

We talked for another ten minutes, then I paid the bill. Aubrey protested but I was firm. "No way are you paying. That's ridiculous."

"Can you afford it?"

That was a fair question but the truth was ironic. "I have more money now than I did when I was in law school. I work forty hours a week."

"I never pictured you as a bartender."

"Me either." Former fraternity president, volunteer, summa cum laude graduate with a list of accomplishments as long as my arms. College prep and law school prep accomplishments. I wasn't sure what those things meant in the real world. "It works for now." It did. If I would stop flirting with customers and drinking on my nights off.

"You look pasty for August. You need to see a little more daylight. We should go for a boat ride."

"I have become a little bit of a vampire. That sounds cool." Taking the ferry had been relaxing, I had to admit.

We walked back up the hill. It seemed weird to me to not always be jumping in a car. Aubrey had offered to drive us down but it didn't seem like a big deal to walk. I liked the heat on my skin. She was right, I'd spent the whole damn summer inside in the dark. In another minute the snow would be flying and I hadn't even enjoyed the summer.

I told myself that was why I offered to walk Chloe home when we got back. Emma was sleeping and even though it was nowhere near dark and Chloe lived within view of the house, I answered Aubrey's curious look with, "I need the exercise. Too much beer and not enough time in the gym. I'm getting a gut."

"Walking another five hundred feet down the road is going to combat a beer gut?"

"It can't hurt."

"You're better off going in the barn. Riker has all his workout stuff there. I'll show you later."

So she was basically telling me no. I couldn't walk Chloe home. She handed some money to Chloe, who pocketed it then glanced over at me. Chloe gestured for me to come with her.

# *meant* for *me*

So there, Aubrey. I shot my sister a triumphant look. Her eyes narrowed and she gave me a look that was clearly a warning. I made a face back. What the hell did she think I was going to do? I wasn't into popping cherries for the hell of it, and it was pretty damn obvious that Chloe was innocent. Then again, people weren't always what they seemed. Maybe she had an active dating life. I shouldn't make assumptions based on her silence.

I opened the door for her. She waved to my sister and stepped out onto the porch. The smile she gave me was shy, but not fearful. She pointed to my stomach. Then gave a thumbs up. My conclusion was she wanted to know how dinner was. It was interesting that she'd managed to figure out how to live her life in a perpetual game of charades.

"Yeah, the pizza was good," I told her. "I needed to eat. Woke up totally hungover this morning."

She nodded in understanding. Or I was just going to assume it was in understanding. It was impossible to know for sure. I followed Chloe down the steps and out onto the walk. She cut across the grass instead of going down the driveway.

"It was stupid to go out last night," I continued, because talking to Chloe was a bit like thinking out loud. Immediately I felt like an asshole for even thinking it, but there was a truth to it, no matter how uncomfortable the thought was. "I knew I was taking that ferry today and yet I was up half the night and drank way more rum than should be legal. What's your poison, Chloe?"

But she just shook her head and I wasn't sure if she didn't have a poison or she didn't want to talk about it.

We walked in silence for a minute, but then she held her hand out, palm up, towards me.

"What?" I asked blankly. I didn't understand what she was doing.

She pulled her phone out of her pocket and shoved it towards me. She hadn't written anything on it and the screen was dark so I still felt clueless. When I didn't take it, she reached out with her other hand, took my hand, and brought it to her phone. "Um…"

Chloe mimicked making a phone call. Then pointed to me and then to her.

"You want my number?" Clearly not for actual phone calls. I didn't want to give her my number. She made me feel… unclean. A waste of space. Like her silent innocence made my worthlessness even more obvious. Which was my problem, not hers, clearly, but whatever. I didn't want to give her my number. "I'm leaving in just a couple of days, Chloe. I probably won't come to Vinalhaven again for awhile."

Her face fell.

It made me feel like the biggest prick ever. I took the phone and found her contacts. "You can text me and tell me what you were doing in Rockland," I said. "And how old you are." If she was eighteen I was out, even for casual conversation. I had to draw the line somewhere and when sober, I was determined no chicks under twenty-one. I couldn't guarantee what the hell I would do drunk, but hey, it was a start.

After entering my number I showed her I had labeled myself as Aubrey's Brother instead of as Ethan. "Just in case you've met a bunch of Ethan's on Tindr," I teased her.

Her expression was censorious.

Well then. Not a jokester. Got it. "No? You should try it. It's great for hook-ups." There I was, being an asshole again, egged on by my own personal discomfort. I was ashamed of my choices, and yes, I had used Tindr as a way to easily meet girls who wanted nothing but a fun night, no attachments. It was like online shopping for sex, and it wasn't illegal.

But Chloe just shook her head. Taking her phone she started typing. A minute later I got a text from her.

*I was in Rockland visiting my aunt and uncle. I'm twenty-one. And I don't do online dating anymore.*

Anymore? Intriguing. And shit, I would not have pegged her for twenty-one. Now the question was, did I continue our conversation out loud or did I text her back? I decided to talk. "Does that mean you have a boyfriend?"

She shook her head with a frown. Then she pointed to me and made a question mark in the air.

"Do I have a boyfriend? No." It was yet another stupid attempt at humor because I was uncomfortable with her. But again, her look of reprimand made me feel small and juvenile.

She texted me.

*Are you gay?*

"No. It was meant to be a joke. A stupid one. And no, I don't have a girlfriend either. I've decided not to torture any unsuspecting women who might be crazy enough to think they want to have a relationship with me."

And that didn't sound even remotely bitter. I put my arm around her shoulder because I felt like I was unintentionally upsetting her. We were already in her driveway. I gave her a side hug. "Thanks for babysitting Emma. She's cute, isn't she?"

She nodded and smiled up at me. Then she opened her mouth and for a brief second I thought she was going to actually say something. But of course, no sound emerged and I wondered if I had actually imagined it. Or maybe it was some form of habit, or the need to try, but she wasn't able to make it happen? I didn't know.

Chloe stepped out of my touch.

I walked her to the front door of her house and she slipped inside with a wave. For a minute, I lingered on the front step, restless. Coming to Vinalhaven had been something I'd put off since Aubrey had given birth. Which was shitty. Two months had already gone by and what exactly had I been doing? I had no good reason for staying away and not supporting my sister and getting to know my niece. It was just more one thing I had fucked up.

Standing there in the warm end of summer breeze, I stared out at the lights of my sister's clapboard house in the distance, then back again at Chloe's. I should get off the porch before she or her father wondered what the hell I was doing. Considering I didn't know, I had no real answer to any questions they might pose. For some reason, I had expected Chloe to continue texting me but my phone was silent in my hand.

As I stepped off the front porch and onto the walkway, the sound of a piano filled the air around me. It was from inside the house and drifting out the open windows. Someone had some talent because that was not "Chopsticks" being banged out on the keys. I glanced back and what I saw through the open window surprised me. The interior had several lights on, and with dusk rapidly falling, it made my view perfectly clear of the living room. It was Chloe at the piano. She wasn't using any sheet music that I could see, but was playing gracefully and confidently. At one point, an older man, presumably her father, appeared in the living room, touching her shoulder briefly as he moved past her. It didn't disturb her at all or break her rhythm.

My own shoulders relaxed as I listened. I didn't know classical music at all, so I had no clue what she was playing, but I could tell when someone sucked and when they didn't. Chloe was damn good and it was soothing. I lingered, not wanting to go back to Aubrey's just yet. Seeing my sister was both awesome and guilt producing. Then again, talking to Chloe was the same on a much smaller scale. Without anyone even criticizing me, I felt reprimanded. Maybe it really was time to get my shit in order. If I was feeling bad when no one was saying a damn word to me, then I knew I was being an asshole.

So step two, along with no screwing girls under twenty-one, was to stop drinking. It was allowing me to drift along making stupid choices and not having to take responsibility. *Hey, it wasn't me, it was the booze.* But the reality was that sure alcohol made all those barriers come down, but I still had to own my behavior.

My phone buzzed in my hand and I quickly glanced down at it, for a split second wanting it to be Chloe, even though it couldn't be her. She was still playing and it wasn't like she could tell Siri to text me. It was Lila. It was a picture of her out for the night, made up sexy night out style, false eyelashes on, cleavage on full display. She was making a duck face at me. Well, at the camera. There was no actual message included with the photo. I guess it was meant to say everything that needed to be said. As in, "Look at me, I'm hot."

She was reminding me of her existence. I'd seen it before, even though I didn't exactly understand it. Lila had been angry with me, offended by my attitude. So why didn't she just let me disappear, fade away? Why did she feel the need to make sure we had a repeat of our night together? Was it because she was subconsciously ashamed of having a one-night stand? Was it the need to win? She had to know for her own ego that she could score my attention? I didn't know. I did know that I had no desire to see Lila again.

Step three. Celibacy?

That wasn't an appealing thought. I wasn't sure I could do it. I was tense enough. Without sex I might explode. But I had spent all of my teen years with blue balls and I could do it again. I wanted sex to mean something again and if I needed to get some relief I'd just jerk off.

I texted Chloe.

*You play beautifully. What is that?*

I stole another glance at her. She was absorbed in her playing, her hair falling forward to cover her face. For the first time in forever, I was genuinely interested in what a girl was thinking. What was going on in her head? Was it like a running stream of desperate thoughts? Did she want to just scream and be heard and nothing could come out? Was she smart, funny, sly? It was hard to tell.

I wanted to hear her.

Walking away rapidly, realizing if I got caught now it would really be fucking weird since it had been ten minutes, I started a search on my phone on selective mutism. Aubrey had given me the overview, but I wanted more information. Scanning and reading quickly, I discovered that a lot of children with the disorder were artistically gifted. Chloe certainly had that trait.

The article emphasized that these children wanted to speak, but couldn't because of crippling anxiety. Chloe didn't look anxious to me, and she wasn't technically a child anymore. There didn't seem to be a lot of information on what happened when these kids grew up. Did it just mysteriously fix itself? I wondered if it was all at once or if it happened gradually.

That would be pretty damn amazing.

Current studies seemed to show that it wasn't the result of trauma in most cases. That was good to know. I'd had it in my head that mutism came from witnessing a murder or from being raped as a kid. Like serious hard-core, mess you the fuck up trauma. I didn't want to know that Chloe had been through something like that. There were articles on treatments but I was already back at Aubrey's. Her front door was unlocked and I went right in.

"You should lock your door," I told her as a greeting. "Especially with Riker gone."

"I didn't realize you were going to be gone so long," she said mildly, lying on the couch and watching TV. "That's a five minute walk. You've been gone for almost half an hour."

"Is Emma asleep?" I asked, looking around and seeing no drooling and cute baby. I wasn't going to react to her comment.

"Yes." Aubrey yawned. "I'm not sure how much longer I'll last myself. Once she's out, I'm usually out right after her."

I flopped down into a chair opposite her. "You don't care if I stay up, do you? I haven't gone to bed this early since fifth grade."

She made a face. "No. I don't care. But before I go to bed I need to ask you to stay away from my babysitter."

My eyebrows shot up. "Excuse me? I'm not the big bad wolf,

for fuck's sake. I walked her home, that's it."

Aubrey gave me a skeptical look. "Four years ago I would have believed you. Now, I'm not so sure."

Nothing she was saying was surprising. Or untrue. But it still pissed me off. "Chill out. I just find her interesting because of the whole lack of speech thing."

"She's not a circus side show."

"I never said she was!" I kicked my shoes off, annoyed. "For the record, Chloe is the one who asked me for my number, not the other way around."

Her nose wrinkled. "That's because she never gets off this island. You look good to someone who lives in isolation."

That was so rude I couldn't help but laugh. "Wow, hold back on the flattery there. I might get a big head."

"You know what I mean."

"What, that I'm ugly? I'm no pretty boy model, but my face probably won't shatter mirrors." I had no problem getting women. None. I didn't think that I looked good to Chloe because she was chilling in Plato's cave her whole life. She had said she online dated.

Aubrey rolled her eyes. "I never said you were ugly. But she isn't experienced enough to know that you're unavailable. Emotionally unavailable, I mean."

"Okay, Mom," I said, irritated. "Thanks for working your psych degree on me. It's the only use you've got for it I guess."

"Don't get bitchy with me," she said mildly. "Or you'll just confirm that you know I'm right."

I threw a couch pillow at her. "Whatever. So what are we doing tomorrow? If I'm left sitting around all day I might be tempted to sweep your babysitter off her feet."

"Haha, you're hilarious. Want me to have Caitlyn over?"

My chest tightened. "Sure," I said mildly. No point in dragging it out. Twenty months was long enough. Maybe a five minute conversation with Caitlyn would cure me of my emotional unavailability. Not.

I stood up, planning to get a beer in the kitchen. I stopped short, realizing what I was doing. Stress at meeting up with Caitlyn had automatically made me want to reach for a beer. Not to mention it was about the time most nights I started drinking. That kind of scared the shit out of me. I sat my ass back down so fast Aubrey gave me a weird look.

"What's wrong?"

"Nothing. I just remembered something."

"Okay, freak," she said skeptically, in a voice only a sister could get away with. "I'm going to bed. I'll get you a blanket and some towels. I'm sorry you have to sleep on the couch, but Emma took over the spare room. Which was never a guest bedroom anyway, so I don't know what I'm talking about." She gave a laugh as she stood up. "God, baby brain. People say that and it's no joke, I'm telling you."

"They also say girls steal their mother's beauty and that's clearly not true." I gave Aubrey a charming smile.

She laughed. "There's the old lady charmer douchebag I remember from most of my life. Good to have your politician in the making personality back for a brief second."

At one time if not specifically political aspirations I had definitely envisioned myself running for judge in the future. But not now. If I did, a parade of coeds would be trotted out to commentate on my drunken behavior. I hadn't done anything illegal. I hadn't cheated on a woman or been caught with a hooker, but I still didn't think it would go over well if half of UMaine came forward and said they'd hooked up with me. As Aubrey headed to bed, I wondered how many girls I had banged. I had never stopped to think about it or count. I didn't want to.

My phone buzzed. It was Chloe, finally answering me. She must have finished playing.

*It was Pachabel. I'm playing at a wedding in a few weeks.*

Right. The song used for the bride's coming down the aisle. I thought it had sounded familiar. Before I could respond she texted again.

*So you heard me?*

*Yes. I heard you.*

Suddenly that seemed very important.

# chapter
## five

WHO IS GETTING MARRIED?

It was a stupid question to ask because I didn't know anyone in Vinalhaven but I didn't know how else to extend the conversation. I was willing to admit talking to the mute girl seemed more interesting than watching a crap show on TV.

*A local couple.*

I sat there, wondering what the hell I should say to that. I wanted the conversation to keep rolling. But before I could respond she texted again.

*It's an easy piece. I don't need to practice really but I like it.*

On someone else that might have sounded arrogant but it didn't from Chloe.

*How long have you been playing?*

*Since I was five. My parents wanted me to be good at something.*

*You obviously are.*

*I'm not bad. They tried piano and soccer and I was terrible at sports, so piano won.*

*I played soccer. I bet you weren't that bad.*

*Really, really terrible. I'm not competitive. In the orphanage I was always last for everything.*

Shifting on the couch, I stared at my phone screen. The orphanage? So Chloe was adopted. Maybe that explained a whole lot more about the mutism.

*You're adopted?*

*Yes. When I was three. From Russia. I forget not everyone knows that. It seems like everyone does.*

*Do you remember being adopted?*

*Yes. I remember everything.*

Somehow I didn't doubt that. I pictured Chloe's mind like a fishing net- the tide washed everything in as a steady stream but nothing could leave again. It was all trapped inside.

*Do you miss Russia?*

*No. It was cold in the orphanage and no one gave a shit about us. But there is one thing I miss.*

For some reason I hadn't expected Chloe to swear, which was stupid. Of course she swore. Everyone swore. I pictured her as a tiny toddler, malnourished, shivering, her hair dark, skin fair. Huge pale eyes.

*What is that?*

*It doesn't matter.*

But it did. To Chloe. And to me.

*Do you still speak Russian?*

The minute I hit send I wanted to kick the crap out of myself.

She didn't fucking speak English. It sounded like an insult or something.

But before I could apologize Chloe responded.

*I had a hard time learning English at first. But I think in both Russian and English now.*

I wasn't even sure what that meant. I wished I could at least see Chloe's face, read her expressions when she typed her thoughts. Texting could never replace conversation and I felt frustrated. I wanted to hear what she had to say. Yet I couldn't. Never would. Was that why it mattered, because I couldn't have it?

No. That wasn't all there was to it. I wasn't that much of an asshole. She was just frankly the most interesting girl I'd met in years. It wasn't just that she was mysterious. It was why she was mysterious. She had a life that set her apart, made her different. Cerebral. She didn't spend her days taking selfies and having vapid pointless chatter with girlfriends or random girls. Her thoughts mattered and her speech, because it was almost nonexistent, mattered most of all.

Or maybe her speech didn't matter one iota. It was intriguing and strange and a welcome distraction from my own self-created bullshit.

Which was why I sent the next text.

*Can I see you?*

*What do you mean?*

*Let's go for a walk on the beach or go into town for a drink.*

I stared at the ellipse indicating she was typing a response, wanting her to say yes. Aubrey's house was small and quiet and it suddenly felt like the walls were closing in on me. I wanted, needed to walk. I couldn't go to bed this early. My schedule was too far off normal hours for turning in at ten at night and I knew I would just toss and turn on the couch for three hours. I could have a couple of beers to help me settle down and sleep but I had just pledged to lay off the booze. I couldn't break that vow an hour in.

Plus there was no denying I wanted to see Chloe.

*Come to my house and we can walk to town. My dad will freak out if I just go by myself. He thinks I'm an easy target.*

There was an eyerolling emoji at the end of her text.

But I had to side with her father on that one. She was an easy target. Would Chloe be able to scream if someone snagged her? Probably not if anxiety caused her lack of speech.

*Okay. I'll be right over.*

I sat up and went into the kitchen. There was a key rack hanging by the back door and I fished Aubrey's keys off the hook and experimented with all of them until I found the one that locked the back door. I didn't want to leave Aubrey and Emma in an unlocked house. Then I left her a note that just said, "Went to town," on the couch in case she came looking for me.

Aubrey was right. It was only a five minute walk to Chloe's. Three because I was really hauling ass. I didn't want Chloe to change her mind. Taking the steps two at a time, I knocked softly on the back door. I figured if she was telling her father what she was doing, he was going to want to see my face. Wishing I had bothered to shave, I rubbed my hand over my jaw. Talking to adults had always been easy for me, but now that I was an adult myself I hadn't had much use for polite conversation. I was the bartender not the law student.

But when an older guy opened the door and eyed me up

and down, I smiled naturally. "Hi, I'm Ethan Walsh, Aubrey's brother." I stuck my hand out.

He took it and shook. "Paul Rush."

"Nice to meet you. Is Chloe here, sir?"

"Yeah, she's here." He paused and continued to assess me without moving out of the way. "Why do you want to see my teenage daughter at ten o'clock on a Wednesday?"

At twenty-one Chloe was not what anyone would call a teenager but I wasn't going to argue with him. "We are going to go into town for a cup of coffee." That sounded better than drinking, which I was determined not to do. The thought of getting hammered then saying or doing something completely assholish in front of or to Chloe made me shudder inwardly. "I'll keep her safe, I promise."

Paul glanced behind him like he was checking to see where his daughter was. Then he stepped out onto the porch with me and pulled the door shut behind him. Wary, I stood my ground, refusing to back up. Paul was a big guy but he had no reason to be suspicious of me. His bulky frame invaded my space, his expression serious.

"My daughter is very naïve," he said in a low, even voice. "And she doesn't spend a lot of time alone with guys. But don't think that because she doesn't talk and is shy that she can be taken advantage of, you understand me? Because she tells me everything and I'll know and then you'll wish you were never born."

Hey, I could respect that he was trying to protect his daughter. I'd known Chloe for eight hours and I already saw that she inspired that same urge in me. Which was a welcome change from what I'd been feeling lately, which was a whole lot of fucking nothing.

"I understand. I have no intention of taking advantage of Chloe. She's not my type of girl," I told him honestly. She was about as different from Lila as you could get. "I'm here as a friend, nothing more. I'm going back to Orono in a few days but I'm a bartender and I'm used to late hours. I don't want to disturb Aubrey and the baby so I figured I'd get out of the house."

That was all true. I wasn't going to start something with Chloe. That would be my shittiest move ever. On the very long list of dickish decisions that would come in top five. Maybe even number one depending on how far I would take it. But I wasn't going to take it or her or anything. I just wanted to have a conversation, like real people did. Like friends.

Except for the fact that Chloe didn't talk.

Paul nodded, slowly. "I'm going to believe you because I'm guessing you have access to girls who are more your type. You look like the guy girls drop their panties for, and I've got no opinion on that. I did my share of chasing ass when I was your age. But my daughter isn't to play with and she's not a circus freak, so if what you're looking for is to be entertained, you might as well go home."

I got it. And it annoyed me that he wasn't letting it drop. I narrowed my eyes. "With all due respect, I think Chloe is probably pretty interesting aside from her body and her disorder. But it sounds like you don't think so."

Maybe I was pushing it, but seriously, come on. If he talked like that in front of Chloe it was no wonder she was anxious.

His eyebrows shot up. "You got balls, I'll give you that. And

Chloe is very interesting. But almost no one bothers to find that out."

The front door flew open. Chloe had a look of alarm on her face and she shook her head and pursed her lips at her father.

"Don't look at me like that," he said mildly. "Ethan and I were just talking."

She pointed to the door and then to her father. Her finger came up and wagged at him. He didn't look particularly concerned about her reprimand.

"Though I have been showing him baby pictures of you," Paul said. The look of horror she gave made her dad laugh. "I'm kidding. Kidding."

Chloe sighed. Her cheeks were stained pink. She looked at me, then her eyes darted away.

"She was a cute baby," Paul said. "In all the pictures she is so damn serious."

Chloe went on tiptoes and covered Paul's ear with her hand. It seemed like she was whispering to him but whatever she said it was quick. He just nodded then kissed the top of her head.

"Have fun and don't stay out too late. Call me if you need anything." Paul gave me a stern look. "Make sure she gets in the house okay. Don't be one of these idiots who lets a girl wander around by herself in the dark."

"I'll make sure she gets in the house, don't worry." I put my hand out. "Goodnight."

He gave me a firm shake.

Paul stayed on the porch while Chloe and I went down the stairs. She was wearing the same clothes as earlier but she had a sweatshirt tied around her waist. I studied her profile. I could see the Eastern European heritage now. It explained the slender and elegant nose, the delicate melon colored lips, the pale blue eyes. I wondered what it must have been like to be three years old, yanked away from everything you knew, thrust onto a plane, taken to strangers, all while everyone spoke a language you didn't understand. It must have been terrifying. Like a nightmare.

It didn't matter how much the adults had been trying to reassure her, she wouldn't have understood what was happening. Or when she was going home. How did you convey without speech to someone that they were being given a new home? A new life.

"Do you have a curfew?" I asked.

She frowned and shook her head. She pointed to her chest and drew the numbers 2 and 1 in the air. 21. She was twenty-one years old. Apparently that meant she didn't need a curfew. Yet she lived at home.

"Do you go to school? College?"

She typed on her phone and showed it to me. *Online. I'm a junior.*

"What are you studying?"

*English.*

That was ironic. To say the least.

We were walking down the hill, towards town. "You don't mind walking, do you?"

She shook her head.

"I studied international and maritime law as an undergrad. I went to law school." I wasn't sure why I bothered to tell her that. It wasn't like I'd graduated and become a lawyer. But it just seemed like part of my history, so relevant. For years, becoming an attorney had dominated my plans. I had wanted the suit, the prestige, the paycheck. But mostly I had wanted the challenge. I wanted to sort and puzzle out cases. Strategize how to win them. It was like a game to me, and one day I had stopped caring about the outcome.

It was like when your favorite football team dominates your thoughts and Sundays for years and then one weekend you're on vacation and then you wonder why you cared so much. Why it mattered to win.

Which would have been fine if I'd had a backup plan. A replacement.

It seemed dishonest to not tell her the full story so I elaborated. "I didn't graduate. So I don't practice law. I just wasn't… ready for it." I wasn't sure if that was the whole truth or not, but it had at least a kernel of truth to it.

Chloe didn't say anything but she reached over and touched my arm, a barely there, split second touch that gave me more comfort than any expressions of sympathy, or words of encouragement, or curious questions could have done. Everyone had an opinion about my dropping out of school and usually it was negative. A glance at Chloe showed no judgment on her face. Nor was it pity. Just compassion, understanding. It amazed me how expressive her eyes could be. She said more with a simple brief touch and her piercing eyes than some people said with a thousand words.

Or maybe I could project onto her whatever I wanted to be there. Which was a disturbing thought.

The fact that she couldn't speak seemed to encourage me to fill that void. I didn't talk to anyone about my personal life and my fuck ups, yet I heard myself say to her, "I've disappointed myself. Have you ever done that? Just looked at yourself and wondered what in the hell were you doing but you weren't able to stop it? I mean, seriously, dropping out of law school is one thing, but basically I have no plans for what to do instead."

The island had a unique smell, a briny, salty perfume that teased at my nostrils with each soft breeze that came up the hill. It was both an oddly isolating feeling being in Vinalhaven yet at the same time I felt less pressure, more at peace here. I was pretty sure that no one in this town gave two craps if I had a degree or not. They would care if I paid or didn't pay my bar tab and whether or not I was going to screw their daughters, but probably not much else. Prestige was measured by different barometers and for the first time as I pulled the door open to the coffee shop and let Chloe enter, I could see why Aubrey was happy here.

There would be no scramble to impress anyone. Everyone did their own thing. Live and let live.

All three heads of customers in the shop swiveled and looked at us. Two waved, not at me, but to Chloe. But then they went back to what they were doing. One guy had a laptop in front of him. The couple in their fifties were reading the newspaper and appeared to be doing the crossword. The barista was messing around with the espresso machine behind the counter. She was in her twenties and cute. She gave me an assessing look as we approached the register.

"Hi, can I get a regular coffee?" I turned to Chloe. "What would you like?"

"She wants an iced caramel macchiato," the girl said. "Right, Chloe?"

Chloe nodded.

I wondered if she really did or if it was just easier to always have the same thing so communication was easier. Pulling my wallet out to pay, I noticed Chloe was digging in her pocket. "No, I've got it."

The barista glanced back and forth between us. "So, Chloe, who is your friend?" she asked. "Tell me all about him."

It seemed mean-spirited to me, considering she obviously knew Chloe couldn't answer. Her eyes were shrewd, the tilt of her head making it clear she knew exactly what she was doing. I had spent enough time around mean girls to recognize the signs, the passive-aggressive intent to humiliate.

"I'm Aubrey Riker's brother," I told her. "And Chloe's friend. That's all you need to know." I could play the asshole if she wanted to be a bitch. I'd had plenty of practice the last year. Handing her a twenty, I raised my eyebrows in a clear challenge. "Keep the change." I glanced at her name tag. "Emily."

It didn't seem to faze her. If anything, she looked intrigued. Excited.

God, why was the male-female dynamic so fucked up? She should be running as far away from me as possible. Yet instead she asked, "So how long are you in town, Aubrey's brother and Chloe's friend?"

"A few days." Then in a clear dismissal I turned to Chloe. "Want to grab a table while I wait for the drinks?"

"I'll bring them out to you," Emily said. "Go ahead and sit down."

"Great, thanks." I followed Chloe to a table and sat down across from her. "You friends with her?" I asked in a low voice.

She shook her head.

"She seems kind of snarky or something. Or maybe I'm just imagining that."

Another head shake. Chloe pulled her phone out. She typed then held it out for me.

*Bully.*

"Ah, that makes sense. She has that look about her. Grade school or later?"

She nodded.

"All of it?"

A thumbs up.

"Charming." I glanced over at Emily. Pick on the mute girl. Nice. But I couldn't ask Chloe to tell me about it. Being with her was both oddly comforting and frustrating as hell. I felt like I'd met the first girl in years I was actually interested in getting to know and she couldn't tell what was in her head. That was ironic, to say the least.

Chloe shrugged. Then she typed again.

*Were you ever picked on?*

I shook my head. "No, not really. Though I wasn't a bully either. I was the guy who got along with everyone. I have no complaints about my childhood at all."

So what went wrong?

She didn't type that or ask it but I could see the question on her face.

"Maybe when I realized that wanting something wasn't enough to be able to have it," I said, as if she'd actually asked the question. "But now that I even say that out loud it doesn't feel true. I don't know." I had fallen in love and for the first time ever I'd been well and truly gutted. It would have been easier to deal with if it had been something like not getting in to the law school I wanted. Instead it had been my stupid sad sack of a heart that had been stomped and I had felt… small. Like a loser. I had offered everything and it hadn't been enough and for the guy who had really never failed in any major way, it had sent me reeling.

"I know, poor Ethan, right?" I scoffed. "It has not been a rough life. So why am I such a fuck up? I don't have that answer either, Chloe." I gazed at her. "You're wasting your time hanging out with me. I have nothing to offer."

Chloe pursed her lips.

Emily came over to us and put our drinks on the table. She was swinging her hips and she tossed her hair and gave me a smile. I gave her an absentminded, "Thanks," wondering what Chloe had been about to say. Then being unnerved to realize it mattered to me. I wanted her approval for some reason.

When Emily turned and left, Chloe pushed her phone to me. Her typing speed was unreal. I guess it was out of necessity.

*Friendship isn't about what's in it for me. I like talking to you. And you have more to offer the world than you give yourself credit for.*

"How do you know?" I asked, feeling moody and melancholy. The craving for a shot of whisky was strong and unbidden.

Chloe just smiled.

It was a confident, peaceful smile.

For someone Aubrey claimed was riddled with anxiety causing her to be unable to speak, Chloe seemed to me one of the most at peace people I'd ever met. She was shy, but she looked me in the eye, and she seemed happy. At the least content with who and what she was. Her role in the world.

I didn't know what my role was.

"Do you actually like playing the piano?" I asked, the question randomly popping into my head.

She nodded.

"I don't like anything," I said. "Nothing matters."

That was the root of all my problems. I didn't give enough of a shit about anything to make any sort of effort anymore. I was used up at twenty-five.

Chloe typed.

*You matter.*

As I read the words on the screen she thrust at me, they hit me like a semi-truck speeding down the highway. My gut clenched.

Did I?

I wasn't even sure.

# *chapter*
## six

"THANKS FOR COMING OUT WITH me," I said, avoiding her comment. "I'm a night owl because of my job. I can't go to bed this early. And I'm kind of an insomniac anyway." When I wasn't drinking, that is. I slept like the dead when I was drinking. Which probably was technically called passing out.

Chloe nodded then made like she was passing her hands over the piano keys.

"You play to fall asleep?" When she nodded I grinned. "I bet that thrills your parents, and your sister, right?"

She smiled back.

*My little sister hates it, but my dad doesn't mind.*

I'd seen her father's protectiveness. That was a man who loved his daughter. He probably worried a lot about her future. Maybe he liked the piano playing and maybe he didn't, but he probably wasn't about to stop her from doing something she enjoyed.

"My parents have washed their hands of me," I said. "They figure I'm old enough to figure my own shit out and I don't even see them that often. I probably should make more of an effort." I sipped my coffee and stared down at my hand. My thoughts were jumping from one thing to another. Being with Chloe was like a weird stream of consciousness thinking out loud. I had bursts of verbal vomit, then I'd become aware of it and try to ask her questions, draw out information about her. It took more thought, effort to be with her. But that wasn't necessarily a bad thing. Everything had been too easy for me. "I thought about getting another tattoo the other day," I said randomly.

Her eyes widened.

"I have one on my calf, which maybe you saw, and a couple on my chest, my bicep. Got them all in the last year, but none are visible when I'm wearing a shirt, even a T-shirt. I thought this week that maybe I should just accept that this is what I am, this is what I'm doing. I'm a bartender. I can show a tattoo, hell, it's almost expected. I shouldn't be holding off because in the back of my head I'm thinking that I'm still going to get some kind of corporate job."

Yet I wasn't ready to give that up. I knew that. I wasn't ready to close the doors entirely on any white collar job. Yet I wasn't doing anything to change a damn thing. All I knew for sure was that I was a walking disaster. A hot fucking mess.

*Why don't you know what you want?*

Chloe's latest typed words were so stark, so obvious. Maybe her inability to speak let her cut through all the bullshit and politeness and small talk and just ask flat out straight up, what in the fucking hell do you want?

"Maybe I haven't seen what I want yet," I said, eyeing her.

She tucked her hair behind her ear. Her mouth opened and for a second I expected words to come out. They didn't.

"What does your voice sound like?" I asked, before I could stop myself. It felt like I was seeing only half of who she was. Would her voice be high, low, soft, melodic? Sexy? The curiosity was only growing the more time I spent with her.

She should have been offended. It was a rude question, even if I hadn't intended to be rude. But Chloe just shrugged.

*Normal. Even if I'm not normal.*

I didn't like that every time she typed her thoughts her head had to drop down to view the keyboard on her screen so I hadn't seen her eyes when she articulated her feelings. Then when I read them I still wasn't looking at her. It was an odd screen between me and her that I'd never experienced. Maybe with someone else I wouldn't have cared, but it seemed to matter with Chloe.

"You're normal. Or maybe you're not. But who wants to be normal? Normal people are petty and selfish and generally shitty. Like me."

Without warning, Chloe shoved her chair back and stood up. Stomping over to the trashcan I watched in astonishment as she tossed her drink, which was still half full, then went and stood at the door to the coffee shop. Apparently we were leaving. She looked pissed off, and I wondered what I had said that had honked her off. Slowly, I rose too and picked up my cup. I was taking mine with me. Though caffeine wasn't going to help my sleep issues.

"Is something wrong?" I asked. "I thought you didn't have a

curfew."

She wrinkled her nose at me. Then surprising me even further she made a fist with her small hand and punched me in the bicep.

"What?" I asked in astonishment. "I don't understand."

Chloe made a sound in the back of her throat that was pure exasperation. But then she whirled and shoved the door open and strode out onto Main Street, letting the door slam in my face. I glanced around to see if anyone had noticed her odd behavior. Emily was watching with a smirk on her face. I raised my eyebrows in her direction. She shrugged. "Good night," she called out. "Tell Crazy Chloe there's a bonfire down at the beach Friday and she's welcome to come, but only if she brings you."

I frowned at her in disgust, then shoved the door even harder than Chloe had. She was sitting on the window ledge in front of the shop. Her hair was falling forward, hiding her face. "We going home?" I asked.

She nodded.

"I'm sorry if I offended you in some way."

She shook her head.

God, I'd never realized how irritating body language could be. I wanted to shake her and make her talk. Like if I rattled her shoulders the words would jar loose and she could tell me what the fucking hell was going on in her head.

But she couldn't. And I wouldn't. So I held my hand out to her, breathing deeply to calm my suddenly jagged nerves. "I want a drink," I said flatly. "And I'm probably an alcoholic. I feel like I suddenly want to stick my face in a mixing bowl full of vodka and suck it up like its Jell-O. That is fucked up, isn't it?"

She nodded.

But then she took my hand and stood up. Chloe shifted into my space and her free hand came up to gently cup my cheek. No, she mouthed.

The silent entreaty made my gut twist.

When she drew her hand out of mine and wrapped her arms around my neck, I sank into the hug she was offering. I closed my eyes and breathed in her sweet scent. She felt lithe and fragile in my arms and I felt big, clunky, like I could crush her and there would be no fixing it. No repairing the damage.

But I didn't pull away. I couldn't pull away.

It was the first honest embrace I'd had in almost two years. "You're right," I said gruffly in her ear. "You're not normal. Because if you were you'd run away from me as fast as possible, not hug my sorry ass."

I could feel her smile, her breath tickling my skin with a soft sigh.

We walked back to her house, her hand back in mine. I hadn't held hands with such innocence since I was seven.

Only I'd be lying if I said I wasn't attracted to her. I was, but that attraction felt wrong. Dirty. Like I was doing the worst thing ever in the history of worst things if I turned our interaction into something sexual. It would be the ultimate dick move. So it was innocent. Sort of.

At her house, I squeezed her hand and said, "Goodnight, Chloe. Thanks for hanging out with me." I didn't know why she'd gotten angry or upset, but maybe it didn't matter. She'd tell me if she wanted me to know. What I did know was I wanted to see her again. "That chick at the coffeeshop said there's a bonfire at the beach Friday night. Want to go with me? I'm leaving Saturday."

For a second, she stood in the doorway of her house, the lamplight of the living room framing her face, making her expression difficult to read. But then she nodded.

"Okay, cool." I backed up on the porch.

She tapped her wrist, like she was wearing a watch then made a question mark in the air.

"I don't know. Nine?" I didn't have any actual details but maybe Aubrey would know. "And maybe I'll see you tomorrow?" Because posing that as a question wasn't even remotely pathetic. I mentally rolled my eyes. I usually had more game. So I touched the ends of her hair, flipping it upward. "I want you to play the piano for me. A private concert."

She audibly sucked in a breath. Without responding with either a nod or a shake of her head, she just turned and shut the door behind her.

I was left alone on the porch.

My phone had been buzzing in my pocket nonstop. I pulled it out and glanced at it. Pictures from Lila. I could vaguely see her pursed lips in the tiny thumbnail size photo on my screen. I didn't bother to enlarge it. I didn't want to talk to Lila. It was after eleven so I didn't expect Chloe to start playing the piano and she didn't. The light in the living room went out.

Stepping off the porch I kicked a clump of grass with my sandal. I wanted to punch something. I wanted to shatter glass, scream. Drink. Heavily. Until nothing mattered.

But then I remembered Chloe's words.

*You matter.*

# *meant* for *me*

A T AUBREY'S I UNLOCKED THE door and came in the kitchen to find her sitting there leafing through a magazine, Emma nursing. Both of them looked half-asleep and cracked out.

"Hey."

"Hey," she said, glancing back at me with disapproval. "I don't have to ask where you've been, do I? Seriously, Ethan? I have to live here, you know."

My sister's voice sounded sleepy and irritated.

"Whatever," I said, and opened the fridge. My hand was outstretched for a beer when I realized what I was doing and caught myself. I spun around and sat down hard on the other kitchen chair. Emma was making little sounds of contentment. I reached out and petted the back of her head, wanting to feel her soft hair.

Then I realized how close I was to Aubrey's nipple and really wanted that drink again.

"We went for coffee. I told you, I can't go to bed this early. It's impossible. What's the big deal?" Even as I said it, I knew what the big deal was. I knew exactly what the problem was.

"Don't play stupid, it's lame." She blew her hair out of her eyes. "But okay. You're clearly going to do whatever you want. And I can't really say much about that. I've been known to do that myself."

"Thanks. I guess." I rubbed my jaw. "I don't want to hurt Chloe. And I swear I'm not playing with her for my own amusement. I'm just… drifting, Aub. I don't know what I'm doing. Then I see someone like her and I think, she manages to figure her shit out, but I can't? It's stupid."

"Ethan. No one has their shit figured out. This is a fact. Are you happy bartending? If you are, then fuck 'em."

"I don't think happy is the right word for it. I'm managing."

Emma had fallen asleep and Aubrey was shifting her.

"Want me to take her and put her in her crib?" I asked.

"Sure. I'm not going to turn down anything that can allow me to go back to bed faster." She kissed Emma's head. "Goodnight, angel, sleep until morning and have sweet dreams." She kissed her again. "That one is from Daddy."

It made me ask the question I'd been curious about. "Are you happy? With Riker?"

Her face relaxed and her voice went soft. "Yeah. Very happy."

"Good." That was all I needed to see and hear. It was clear she was and my throat tightened. I was glad to hear it. If I was honest, I was jealous too. Petty, but there it was. I took Emma from her and cradled her. Her arms and legs were slack. "How is a baby this small so heavy? She feels like a box of lead." It was amazing that she didn't even react to the transfer at all. Her breathing was soundless, her lips still sucking in her sleep.

"She's pretty packed solid, I have to admit." Aubrey yawned and stood up. "I'll see you tomorrow." She shuffled out of the kitchen.

Testing Emma's weight in my arms, I settled her into a better hold and followed my sister down the hall. Emma's nursery had a stars and moon glowing nightlight on one wall, giving the room a soft glow. It had a jungle theme and I deposited Emma down onto a zebra striped crib sheet. Leave it to Aubrey to be anti-pink. "Goodnight, kid. I hope you don't dream a lion is chasing you." There wasn't a blanket in there, but I figured it was summer. She wasn't going to get cold.

With one last slide of my finger over her silky, plump cheek I retreated. In the hallway I looked at my phone and saw that Chloe had texted me links to several videos. Curious, I went to the couch and sank down, clicking the first one. It was Chloe playing at some kind of recital or event.

It amazed me that she felt comfortable sending that. Her insecurity or anxiety or whatever it was clearly didn't extend to her abilities as a pianist. Nor did she mind me seeing her play obviously. Plugging my phone into headphones I dug out of my bag, I shoved them in and pushed play. The music filled my ears. It wasn't anything I recognized but I could see that her fingers were crossing the keys rapidly. The music was intense, haunting. But it wasn't really the sound she was producing, though that was extraordinary. It was the confidence she clearly had. It changed her face.

She looked her age in mastery of the piano, mature and beautiful, capable of stirring shit inside me that didn't need to be stirred. I wondered how those delicate and long fingers would feel stroking over my cock. Would she squeeze my shaft and work me soft, then hard, then soft? I started getting an erection and I shifted on the couch. My thoughts weren't supposed to take that detour, but once there, I couldn't shake them. What would her lips feel like on mine? Would she make a sound if I ate her pussy until she came? It wouldn't be fucking with a girl like Chloe. It would be intimate.

Exactly what I wasn't looking for.

And what I didn't deserve and wasn't entitled to take.

I couldn't give her what she would want or need.

Hell, I didn't even know if she was attracted to me or not. She probably thought I was entertaining but a total tool.

Yet I couldn't stop watching her. Couldn't stop studying her fingers, her cheekbones, her lengthy eyelashes that were visible when I zoomed in on her in the video. She was so beautiful.

After an hour and three more videos that I watched a dozen times each, I finally drifted off into a restless sleep with Chloe in my ears and before my eyes.

I WOKE UP A HALF DOZEN times during the night and when one o'clock the next day rolled around and Caitlyn arrived at Aubrey's, I was in a foul mood. I looked like hell. I felt like hell. The only thing that made the prospect of getting through this stupid social nicety with my ex was the fact that Chloe was coming over at three and we were going to get a late lunch. I figured if we went somewhere to eat it wouldn't be so frustrating that she wasn't talking to me. We'd both have deli meat in our mouths. But first I had to deal with Caitlyn.

She smiled and it seemed genuine as she came into the room. "Hey, Ethan, it's really great to see you." Without any appearance of discomfort, she reached out and hugged me.

I put my arms around her in return and waited to feel some sort of longing or regret. But I didn't really feel anything other than mild nostalgia. She didn't feel like she belonged to me anymore. I remembered her scent, her eyes, yet everything was different. She was then, not now. It wasn't that she seemed like a stranger, but for the first time, I felt truly like both of us had moved on, not just her.

Of course, she had moved on to a real relationship and I was jerking around with the girl of the week.

"Thanks, it's great to see you, too. You look good, Caitlyn."

She stepped back, her smile still broad. "Thanks. So isn't Emma the cutest baby you've ever seen?"

"Definitely." I noted she didn't say I looked good in return. I didn't. I needed a haircut and a shave and about a week solid of sleep. I needed to go back to the gym, get some Vitamin D. It hadn't seemed to matter much before, but now I was aware of how scruffy-ass loser I was. But at the same time, I figured there was no fucking point in worrying about it. It was what it was. So I wasn't exactly Magic Mike. I still had no problem getting ass.

"How are you?"

"Good. Great." She shifted into Aubrey's living room. "I like being back home more than I would have ever guessed."

"It's kind of a cool place. You kept it a secret from everyone. I bet you never thought Aubrey would end up living down the road from you."

I did resent that Caitlyn had kept her entire life basically a secret from me. It shouldn't matter anymore, but it was hard to let that go, that she hadn't trusted me enough to understand I wouldn't give a shit how she had grown up. I hadn't been with her because I thought she came from an upwardly mobile white family from the supposed right neighborhood. I had been with her because she was intelligent and beautiful and a caring person. I knew that she'd felt a certain sense of shame for having grown up poor with a mentally ill mother, but come on. She had been willing to marry me, but not share the truth with me. It was bullshit.

Bullshit I needed to let go. She had made mistakes and I

knew she felt bad about that. I wasn't exempt from bad choices. Obviously.

She made a face and looked a little uncomfortable with my words. "Yeah, I guess that was childish. But I wanted to forget, so yes, it's totally ironic that both Aubrey and I ended up here. And now you're here."

"Just for a few days. It's good to see Aubrey and Emma."

My sister, who was sitting on the couch with the baby, had an expression on her face that was hard to read. I was pretty sure she was worried about me and my reaction. I felt fine. There was still that lingering resentment and I was busted from not getting enough sleep, but it was whatever. I didn't look at Caitlyn as she came in and sat down and feel that same pit in my gut I had for the longest time. I didn't want to grab her and shake her until she acknowledged that we should have been together. Nor did I want to kiss her or have sex with her. There was no attraction really. I felt… neutral.

"How's Heath?" I asked, just to get that out in the open. I didn't want her to feel like she couldn't talk about her boyfriend. "Aubrey says he has a fishing boat. That sounds cool."

"He's great, thanks. The wedding planning is just so ridiculously out of control but it will all be over in two weeks. I think I've figured out weddings aren't my thing." She laughed. Then she caught herself, her cheeks turning red.

Awesome enough, I didn't feel anything at that news. That brought me a huge sense of relief. It was like suddenly realizing the prison door is actually unlocked and you're free. "Two weeks? Congrats. Hey, is Chloe your pianist for the ceremony then?"

My thoughts drifted back to the videos she had sent me. She

had a gift. Watching her play was mesmerizing.

Caitlyn looked surprised. "Yes, she is. How did you know?"

"She told me."

"She was babysitting for me yesterday," Aubrey said.

There was a knock on the front door. My sister stood up and passed the baby to Caitlyn. "Here, hold her." When she pulled open the door, she said, "Speak of the devil. Hi, Chloe."

I sat up straighter and ran my fingers through my hair. Like that was going to do anything to it. It was a shaggy mess, but maybe Chloe was into scruffy guys. Not that it should matter. As Chloe came into the room, her gaze drifted over to me and she gave me a shy smile and a small wave.

A smile played over my lips. Bigger than it should be under the circumstances. "Hey, Chloe. You're early or did I get the time wrong? I do that." I stood up because I felt like I wanted to greet her in a way that wasn't lazy ass on the couch.

She shook her head and pointed to Caitlyn.

"Oh, you're here to see Caitlyn?"

Nod.

Well, that was disappointing. "And here I thought you wanted to see my ugly face."

Chloe blushed.

The satisfaction I felt at that color staining her cheeks was way inappropriate. Not surprising though. I was lying when I told Aubrey my interest in Chloe was entirely cerebral. I was attracted to her. That was pretty fucking obvious.

Chloe typed on her phone and she passed it to me.

*You give good face.*

I laughed.

"Should we leave you two alone?" Aubrey asked.

The bitch was back. Motherhood hadn't robbed my sister of her need to take random jabs at people. I turned to her, irritated. "Yeah, could you? Thanks." Then I rolled my eyes. "Chill out. She said she's here to talk to Caitlyn, but then we're going out to lunch."

Caitlyn was watching us with an open mouth. She looked shocked. "How do you two even know each other?"

"We met on the ferry here." I wondered if she was going to voice an opinion about us spending time together. She had no right to an opinion as far as I was concerned, but that didn't stop Aubrey so maybe it wouldn't stop Caitlyn either.

But Caitlyn didn't seem to know what to say. She just gave an "Oh," and that was the end of that.

There was a time when it would have made me maliciously gleeful to have her aware that a chick was into me. But it wasn't even a thought. I was more focused on getting Chloe to myself. I wanted to talk to her. And yeah, stupid as it was, I wanted to hold her hand again. Crazy. But she was wearing a strapless dress and it looked like she had a bikini top on under it, given the straps that came up around her neck. I was distracted as hell by the idea of her in nothing but a bikini. I wanted to reach over and tug that dress straight on down to her ankles.

I wasn't exactly sure when I had started thinking of Chloe as someone I wanted to kiss and touch and see naked but now that those thoughts were hanging around, I couldn't shake them. They were stronger by the minute.

So I said, "Come sit down," and touched her elbow with a smile.

She smiled back.

And we were just a couple of smiling fools.

"Is everything okay?" Caitlyn asked. "Did you want to talk about the wedding music?"

She shook her head. Typing on her phone rapidly, she handed it to Caitlyn.

Caitlyn read it, her lips moving. "Oh, sure no problem. You know we always have too many."

She looked over and met my eye as Chloe gave a thumb's up and sat down next to me on the loveseat. "Chloe wants to pick some of our raspberries and make some jellies."

I turned to Chloe. "You make jelly? Does that mean you can cook?"

She nodded.

"Chloe is a fantastic cook," Caitlyn said. "Her baking is phenomenal."

Chloe just made a face.

"Wow, you're impressive," I told her, honestly. "You can play the piano and cook like a baller. And beautiful. You're basically the perfect woman."

"Don't tease her," Aubrey said.

"I'm not teasing!" I protested. "I'm being totally fucking serious. Chloe knows I'm serious."

I could tell she believed me because her eyes were glassy and her breathing was uneven. This close to her on the couch, our legs were brushing here and there and she could feel it too, I know she could. The stirring heat between us. The urge to kiss her was intense and I leaned in, just wanting to breathe in her scent. "You know, don't you?"

She nodded. Her lips parted.

For a second I thought she was either going to speak or kiss me, but both were wishful thinking. But it amazed me again how much she could communicate with her eyes. She looked slumberous, innocently lustful. I knew she wanted that kiss I desperately wanted to give her. But Chloe was the girl who would want more. She would want to date, be in a relationship. And I would want more than a kiss too. But what I wanted was different. I wanted to strip her clothes off slowly, stroke and kiss her everywhere. I wanted to touch and taste and turn her on so that she was dripping wet for me. Then I would eat out her pussy until she writhed and yanked on my hair and came hard like no guy had ever made her come. Finally, while she was still catching her breath, I would shove my cock so deep inside her she would be forced to open her mouth and scream her pleasure. She wouldn't be able to stay quiet.

I wanted to do all of that and more, over and over, because Chloe wasn't like any girl I'd ever met and I wanted her with a hot-mouthed thirst that was taking over my thoughts.

But I knew that I couldn't give her more than that. I was not a good boyfriend for a girl like Chloe. Maybe I wasn't a good boyfriend for any girl. Not now. Not when I was still sorting my waste of a life out.

So I wasn't going to kiss her. And she wasn't going to kiss me. Because I was pretty fucking sure I couldn't stop at just a kiss.

"Is it hot in here?" Aubrey asked.

Right. My sister and Caitlyn were in the room. I hadn't forgotten but I hadn't cared.

Caitlyn looked like she didn't know what the hell to think.

She didn't look horrified but she was definitely shocked. My sister was eyerolling so dramatically I was afraid she might fall over backwards.

"Yes," I told her, giving her a look of warning. "It's hot in here. You need air conditioning."

"Pfft," was her response to that. "I don't think that's the issue."

Since my conversation with Caitlyn was going nowhere and I was okay with that, I turned to Chloe and asked, "Want to go to lunch now instead? Are you hungry?"

She nodded.

"Cool." I stood up and held my hand out for her. "Good to see you," I told Caitlyn and I genuinely meant it. I was glad I was able to vanquish that demon. Seeing her wasn't really as traumatic as I'd been making it out to be. It was obvious to me now that the attraction wasn't there anymore. I looked at her and felt very removed, distant. That was liberating as hell. "Congrats on your marriage. I hope the wedding is awesome."

"Thanks, Ethan." Her expression was touched. Tender. "Take care of yourself."

It was weird to know that we had been totally intimate with each other. That her mouth had been on my junk. That she'd cuddled with me in the shower, had lain on my chest naked. That we had meant something to each other and had intended to spend our lives together. I couldn't picture it now. Definitely time to unload that ring resting in my backpack.

"You, too, Caitlyn." I knew that on the island she went by the nickname Cat but she had introduced herself as Caitlyn to me and to everyone at UMaine. To me, she was Caitlyn. I'd never know Cat. Cat was a different person in a lot of ways.

Chloe waved to them.

"When are you coming back?" Aubrey asked.

"I'll be in by dark, Mom, I swear." I made a face at her.

"Dick," was Aubrey's opinion on that.

"You're going to have to curb the potty mouth," I said as Chloe and I walked to the front door. "Or Emma's first word is going to be fuck and that just is not right."

"You aren't right."

"Never said I was." I hadn't been right in a long time.

The door swung door behind us and I squinted in the sunlight.

Chloe squeezed my hand. Okay? She mouthed to me.

"Yes," I said, touched. She knew that wasn't going to be totally comfortable for me. I wondered if she had seen Caitlyn walking and had just decided to crash the party out of concern for me. Or maybe jealousy?

I guess I'd never know, because she wasn't about to tell me. There was that irony again.

"I'm fine," I added.

For the first time in a fucking long ass time, I truly meant that.

# *chapter*
# seven

"WHERE DO YOU WANT TO eat?" I asked Chloe.

She shrugged.

"It's your hood. You tell me."

She mimicked eating something.

"Pizza?" That kind of looked like she was miming taking a bite of a slice.

Nod.

"Okay. I can always eat pizza. Lead the way." As we started walking, I asked, "Were you swimming today?"

She nodded.

"That sounds fun. It's hot as hell in Aubrey's house." I raised my eyebrows up and down. "And I have no idea what Aubrey was implying, by the way."

Her look proved she didn't entirely believe me. But I figured she wouldn't want to address the issue of how we had been checking each other out and I was right.

"It wasn't a big deal to see Caitlyn. I don't know why it seemed like it would be. I guess I was just afraid it would be awkward. But it was fine and I am genuinely happy for her. She and Heath are a better fit than she and I were, truthfully, and the reality is, she was trying to be someone she really wasn't. I cared about that someone. I didn't really know her as well as I thought I did, so how can that be love, you know?"

Chloe nodded.

There it was again. The confessional conversation. I had no idea why I was doing that with her but I was blurting out every freaking thought that entered my head.

Silence unnerved me. I hadn't really realized that before but it was clear that it did. I'd always thought of conversation as vital and I had used words to my advantage, actively participating in college classes, running for president of my fraternity, volunteering as a tutor. Words had been the way I had achieved all of my goals. Speaking up, speaking out. In the last year I had listened more than I had spoken and I wondered suddenly if that were part of the reason I was dipping lower and lower into a dark place. It wasn't my nature to be the brooding bartender in the dark.

So I could talk, but hell, did I have to be treating Chloe like I was sitting in a shrink's office?

For a minute I just lapsed into silence, looking around us as we walked. Then I started talking again. "When I was a kid I wanted to sail around the world, starting right here, off the coast of Maine. I had navigation charts and clippings of articles on guys who had done it. Boats torn out of magazines. I was serious about it, creating a checklist of supplies and charting my course. When I would depart. All of that." I hadn't thought about that in a long time but seeing all the boats in the water had jogged the memory. "I wonder when I forgot about that." I couldn't really remember. Middle school maybe. "Maybe when I discovered girls." I shot a glance at Chloe. "Girls are distracting."

She gave a soft laugh and pointed to me.

"Boys are a distraction too?" I asked, amused. "Or just me?"

Her laughter died and she nodded, gazing up at me.

"Which one?" I murmured.

Chloe's hand rose and her finger lightly jabbed me in the chest.

"So it's me." I shouldn't be so glad to hear that but I was.

We were almost to town, about to descend the hill. There was a soft breeze kicking up Chloe's hair and the air smelled warm, salty. The temptation to kiss her was greater than I could resist. She looked so beautiful, so trusting. There was nothing calculating or manipulative in the way she stared up at me. Her eyes spoke to me and I had to answer.

For a split second, I reminded myself that it was a bad idea to start something I couldn't finish, but it didn't stop me. Covering her finger with my own much bigger hand, I held tight so she couldn't retreat away from me. She knew what I was going to do. She leaned in closer, let her lips part softly in anticipation.

Tipping my head down, I watched her until the very last second when I let them drift half closed. Then I took her lips with mine, my other hand on the back of her head.

Chloe had the softest lips I had ever kissed and our mouths were a perfect fit for each other. I had expected it to be sweet, a quick brush. But she kissed me back with a seductive and aggressive enthusiasm I wasn't expecting. I could hear her breathing, feel her finger scraping across my chest, her body nestling as close to me as she could with our arms trapped between our chests. It felt necessary, required, to tease her lips further open with my tongue so I could dip inside and take the kiss hotter, deeper.

She tasted better than I could have possibly imagined. Sweet and tangy and eager and I started to lose my control, burying my fingers further in her hair, holding her tighter. For a second I broke off and listened to the sound of our mutual ragged breathing, studying her face. Then she tilted her head in such an obvious invitation to take more that I couldn't stop myself. I kissed her hard, sweeping my tongue over her bottom lip, feeling an animalistic satisfaction when she gave a low groan in the back of her throat. This was one way to make her speak, and it was obvious what she was saying. She liked it as much as I did.

I had expected Chloe to be shy, fumbling. But she wasn't. It was like her mouth was meant for me.

"You feel so good," I murmured into her ear.

I let go of her hand and when both our arms dropped she moved into the circle of my arms. Her breasts pushed against me and suddenly I wanted to yank her clothes off and take her with an urgency that almost overwhelmed me. It felt like it had been years since I'd had sex, my cock throbbing against her thigh.

"Chloe," I said, even as I kissed down the graceful slope of her neck and across the top of her breast. "I need to stop." My hands had somehow ended up on her ass and it was a small tight ass that was doing dangerous things to my control. I wanted to pick her up by that perfect backside and set her down onto my cock so I could destroy both of us with passion.

But Chloe couldn't tell me that yes, I should stop. Nor did she step away. Instead she cupped my face in her delicate hands when I lifted my head and kissed me again.

"You're killing me." Covering her hand with mine, I squeezed it hard and took a deep breath and stepped away from her sexy body and those eyes that seemed to offer me anything I could possibly want.

I would have thought that my words would confuse her or she would look apologetic.

Wrong. I was so wrong. She looked satisfied, like she had done her job well.

Which was even sexier.

I narrowed my eyes. "We are going to start walking before I do things I shouldn't and regret."

A small smile danced across her lips.

I suddenly found myself jealous of these mysterious guys she had online dated. I didn't want to think that anyone else had brought Chloe pleasure. That she might have come at the hands of some tool, or rolled her eyes back in ecstasy as she took a cock that wasn't mine.

Those thoughts scared me. What the fuck business was it of mine?

I was leaving the day after tomorrow. That would be the end of my interaction with Chloe.

Her hand slipped into mine and she smiled up at me.

Yeah. I was full of shit if I thought I wasn't going to keep texting with her after I left. It couldn't be anything, but since when had that stopped me?

I would just have to be careful.

Because I couldn't hurt Chloe. That would be the worst crime on my lengthy rap sheet.

W*HILE WE ATE PIZZA I* told Chloe about law school and my failure to do what needed to be done. Mostly she just listened but once she typed on her phone as I was berating myself.

I glanced down at her phone as she slid it across the table to me.

*Stop it. So you didn't want to be a lawyer. Who cares?*

The words were like a slap and I sat back hard in my chair. I guess she was right. Who the fucking hell cared what one Ethan Walsh was doing with the rest of his life? Sure, I was disappointing my parents and myself but no one else cared. I was nothing.

I knew that wasn't the way Chloe meant it, but I couldn't help but feel that impact of irrelevance. All my high school and college years had been spent striving for success. For relevance. What did any of it matter?

"I care," I said in a tight voice.

Contrition crossed her face and I felt bad then for making her feel bad. She was just trying to help.

"I'm sorry, that sounded rude," I told her, reaching across the table to brush my fingers over the back of her hand. "But I actually do still want to be a lawyer."

I did. I realized that fully now. "But I'm afraid I'm missing something I used to have and that I will fail."

There it was. The thing I'd been unable to admit for a year.

# *meant* for *me*

I was afraid that I was going to fail. That life had knocked some of the naïve confidence out of me and I would try and not be successful and I would have wasted all this time and everyone would know. This way, I had walked away and looked like some sort of rebellious bad boy, not just a fucking loser.

The drinking needed to stop. That definitely felt like the strongest choice I'd made in a long time.

*Not trying is failure.*

She was right.

"What do you want to be?" I asked.

Chloe mimicked typing on a keyboard.

"A writer?"

She nodded. It made sense. There couldn't be a lot of career options available to someone who didn't speak. "I bet you have a lot to say."

She laughed, the soft, almost soundless laugh that was unique to her. I wondered what it would be like if suddenly Chloe just started talking a mile a minute and her voice was some random grating high-pitched voice. Or if she would have a Russian accent. I had created sound for her in my own head. When I read her words I gave her a voice that seemed like it would fit her appearance, her personality. What if I was totally wrong? That would be weird as hell.

But I would likely never know.

We lapsed into my silence and it wasn't uncomfortable or awkward. Chloe ate and I ate and she communicated with her eyebrows, her hands, her eyes, her mouth. I felt oddly at peace and I watched her, feeling a whole new appreciation for body language. Every thing she did was intentional, thought out, and

86

I wondered if she were this aware of what her hands, her mouth, her body could do, what would she be like in bed? Amazing, I had no doubt. Intuitive as hell. I wondered if she was a virgin. It seemed like she led a pretty isolated life, but hell, people found a way to bang everywhere.

After we ate, we walked along the docks and watched the fishermen and other boats moving in and out of the harbor. We held hands, which just struck me as truly hilarious. It was like bit by bit Chloe was peeling the layers of badass back on me and turning me into a guy who actually was capable of being a decent boyfriend. Maybe I wasn't totally busted after all.

It was the kind of day that had no purpose, was just a lazy stroll around and do whatever the hell you feel like, but after an hour, I realized that I really needed to spend time with my sister. That was the real reason I was in Vinalhaven. "I need to hang out with Aubrey and Emma," I told Chloe. "But I'll text you later. And we're going to the bonfire tonight, though, right?"

She nodded.

I gave her a kiss, this one soft and brief, not wanting to get carried away. Which I would if she did that thing with her tongue to me again.

"I'll come and get you at nine. Your dad isn't going to freak out, is he?"

She shook her head.

After I walked Chloe home, I went to Aubrey's and had the entertaining experience of changing Emma's diaper. "Is this normal?" I asked Aubrey as she monitored my attempt at wiping up her daughter's butt. "This looks like someone dumped a cup of Christmas Ale in her pants."

Aubrey shook her head. "Gross. Yes, it's normal. She doesn't eat solid food so her poop isn't solid either."

Interesting. "Makes total sense though it never would have occurred to me. How did you know anything about what the hell you were doing? We've never really been around kids. I'd be calling the doctor every day."

"I read books and magazines. And I ask Mom when something freaks me out. She talks me off the ledge. But I don't know. Some of it is just common sense."

"You've always been pretty damn pragmatic." I tossed the baby wipe into the wastebasket next to the changing table while Emma kicked her chubby legs. She nailed me in the arm. I faked a dramatic rearback. "Pow. Good contact, kid."

Aubrey laughed. She was lounging in the rocking chair, inspecting her feet. "My feet look like shit. Will you give me a pedicure?"

That made me snort. "Yeah, that's baby brain rearing its insane head because there is no way in hell I am touching your feet. Nor am I your bitch boy."

"You're so selfish."

"Speaking of selfish. While you're crashed out tonight I'm going to some bonfire down on the beach, and I'm borrowing your car, thanks. Don't wait up." I got a fresh diaper back on Emma in some proximity of the right way and snapped her onesie back together at the crotch. I picked her up and gave her chubby cheek a kiss. She turned her head and swiped drool across my mouth. "You're lucky you're cute, because truthfully, you're kind of gross, kid."

"I'm sure that's evolution at work. Make our babies adorable so we don't leave them in the woods. And fine, have fun at the bonfire, but keep in mind most of those people who will be there are five years younger than you. And smoke a lot of weed."

"Sounds like a regular Friday to me," I said, giving her a smirk.

Aubrey shook her head. "When are you going to stop being a douche? I miss the real Ethan, not this Jersey Shore reject."

My jaw set and I settled Emma into the cradle of my arm. "Thanks, Aub. Glad I came to visit so you can be so encouraging."

I knew she meant well but Jesus, why was she always such a balls to the wall bitch?

For that reason, I wasn't about to share with her that I'd just emailed my advisor and asked if it was possible to reenroll for the fall semester that was starting in two weeks. It had been impulsive, yet a long time coming. If I wanted to get my shit together, I couldn't spend my work hours surrounded by booze and girls in very little clothing.

Yet here I was in Vinalhaven heading out to a freaking bonfire keg party with a twenty-one year old.

One fucking step forward, two back.

A KID WHO WAS ASIAN OPENED the door at Chloe's. The little sister, I figured. If Chloe was adopted, maybe the sister was too. Or maybe Chloe's adopted mother was Asian so this kid was their biological child. For the first time I wondered where that mother was. No one ever mentioned her. "Hi, I'm Ethan. Is Chloe here?"

I didn't have a good eye for kids but this one looked like she was about twelve. She was wiry and short and she eyed me curiously. "Yes, come on in. She told me you were coming to get her."

"Did she?" I wanted to ask if she had used her voice or her phone to tell her sister about me. I was also wondering what exactly she had mentioned about me.

"Yep. I'm Sara. Her sister. I guess you can come in."

Her enthusiasm was nonexistent. "Thanks." I stepped into the house after her.

"She's been screwing around with her hair for like an hour," Sara said, her expression showing she thought this was a total waste of time. "And it looks exactly the same as it did before."

That made me laugh. I was guessing Chloe did not want her sister spilling information like that. I also found her attitude amusing. Tomboy, clearly. At least for now. Sara was wearing denim shorts and a t-shirt that was way too big for her. "Chloe is beautiful, she doesn't need to waste an hour, I agree."

"Gross," Sara said. "But she likes you for whatever reason so I guess I have to pretend to like you."

"I don't think you're doing that great of a job," I told her. "But it's okay. Where's your dad, by the way?"

"He's playing poker with other old men."

"Where's your mom?"

"I have no idea. Hell, maybe?" She gave me a saucy grin. "She left five years ago. She got bum kids, cuz you know Chloe doesn't talk and I have ADHD, so she was like peace out and left."

Now that was totally appalling. "Wow, I'm sorry."

She shrugged, twisting the end of her long hair over her finger. "Chloe and me, we're zero for two on mothers, but whatever. Dad tries like twice as hard and he has absolutely no life whatsoever outside of us, which sucks for him, I mean like doesn't he want a lady friend, but we know he'll be there through whatever and it's cool for us, though balls for him."

That was a kid who was fond of run-on sentences. "I'm sure he's glad to have both of you. And poker night."

"True." She flung herself down on the couch and yelled, "Chloe! Your boyfriend is here!"

That made me stiffen. Boyfriend was not a word I liked to have tossed around casually.

Chloe came into the room in an angry flourish, her hair swinging behind her, wearing a bikini top and teeny, tiny denim shorts. Holy shit, that was a lot of skin and a lot of temptation. But she barely even glanced at me. She leaned over the couch and furiously whispered in her sister's ear. Sara made a face.

"Okay, fine, like whatever, but hurry up. He's just standing there waiting for you like a chump."

A chump? She thought I looked like a chump? Sara was the most unnerving combination of savvy old man and rambling tween girl. That must be Paul's influence on her. Plus there was nothing chump-like about me.

A door slammed down the hallway after Chloe rushed off again.

"She talks to me," Sara announced, stating the obvious. "And she's mad at me for telling you she's been watching YouTube video tutorials on getting shiny beach waves in your hair for date night."

This kid definitely had a motor mouth. "You didn't actually tell me that until just now."

"Oops. Sometimes I speak before I think. Chloe has the

opposite problem. So like why didn't it balance out better?"

"Maybe it wasn't supposed to. Maybe Chloe is meant to be the way she is and you're meant to be the way you are."

She sat up. "Are you into karma?" she asked, sounding like she would if she suspected me of believing that alien clowns in drag were set to take over the world.

"I don't think that statement can be classified as believing in karma. I don't think an eye for an eye exists in that if I beat the crap out of my dog, later on a dog will attack me. But I think that we're dealt what we're dealt and we have to just deal."

"Easy for you to say." She rolled her eyes like she was about a decade older than she was.

"Are you sure you're only twelve?"

"Truthfully, not really. I could be ten or eleven or maybe even thirteen. Who is to say that the orphanage even knew? My birthday could be made up, a guesstimate on their part. Is that a real word, guesstimate?"

Before I could answer, Chloe entered the living room. She put her finger up to her lips at her sister.

"I can't help it and you know it," Sara said.

"It's okay," I told Chloe. "She's actually being entertaining."

Chloe rolled her eyes.

"And you look gorgeous, by the way." She did. She had put volume into her hair and she was wearing makeup on her eyes and a gloss on her lips that looked like it would taste like cherries. I wanted to bite it off. She was still in the bikini top and shorts but she'd added a hoodie that wasn't zipped yet. So it allowed me to imagine running my tongue all over that firm, silken skin. She was thin, her tits small and tight and I could see her nipples.

I wanted to cup her breasts and kiss her sweet lips and taste between her thighs.

She blushed a little, but she did look pleased.

Then she shocked me by rushing me and throwing her arms around my neck and giving me a fast, hard kiss. Pulling back, she went to the front door and opened it, tossing me a look over her shoulder that made me instantly hard.

This was going to be a night that was seriously going to tempt my self-control. Which was mostly in shreds anyway.

I waved goodbye to Sara and followed Chloe. If I had any sense I'd pull the plug on what was clearly a date.

But I didn't. She had something I wanted to be a part of, a peacefulness, a confidence, an internal and external beauty. I could barely stand to be alone with my thoughts without alcohol anymore and that was all she was- alone and wrapped in thoughts that would never leave her mouth.

And taking her body wasn't going to give me her thoughts.

# *chapter* eight

*T*HE BEACH PARTY WAS ALREADY underway when we got there. I was right- there was a ton of beer, though no official keg. Aubrey had also been right in that I could smell weed everywhere as we crossed the sand to the noisy group of about twenty people hanging out around a bonfire. I was conscious of the fact that the girl in the coffee shop had basically been a dick about Chloe and I wasn't entirely sure if she was welcome or not. I could give two shits if anyone wanted me there or not. But I didn't want Chloe's feelings hurt and my idea that maybe I would be helping her socially by taking her seemed arrogant as hell and potentially disastrous.

But a few girls and a guy waved and greeted Chloe when we came up. A dude with hair to rival an 80s hair band member stuck his hand out. "Yo, what's up, I'm JC. You're Aubrey's brother, right?"

"Yes, I'm Ethan. Nice to meet you."

"Chloe, you need a beer, dawg."

JC made me feel like I'd fallen into a spoof of how teens talk. He just couldn't be fucking serious. But he was smiling and he seemed nice enough. Chloe took a beer, which for some reason surprised me. Which was stupid. I couldn't keep thinking of her as some innocent little kid while at the same time wanting to bang her brains out. She was an adult. She just didn't talk.

I shook my head when he offered me a beer too. "No thanks. I'm a bartender and on my days off I don't drink." That wasn't the whole truth but it seemed to keep him from making an issue out of it.

Then I realized I didn't have to justify my sobriety to anyone.

Someone was playing bad guitar on the other side of the fire and I felt weary looking around. What was there here for me? I would have preferred walking on the beach alone with Chloe.

Unless I drank, which I wasn't going to do.

I wandered around and made small talk by Chloe's side, made more laborious because she didn't talk. The coffee shop girl Emily made an effort at flirting with me that I found irritating. Chloe had turned to look at some pictures on a blond girl's phone and Emily sidled up alongside of me.

"So, do you want to do a shot with me?" she asked, pulling a flask out of the waistband of her bikini. "I hate the taste of beer but I heart jager."

"Of course you do," I said, unable to fully contain my sarcasm. What did she want, some sort of cool girl badge for walking around with a flask in her bottoms? That jager was probably warm on top of it all. Not appealing.

*meant* for *me*

She pulled a pout. "No? Boo. Don't be boring."

"I'm very boring."

"You don't look boring. You look hot." She reached out and touched my chest.

I was wearing a black t-shirt and cargo shorts. Nothing exciting. She fingered the medallion I wore under my shirt before tugging it out by the chain. My eyebrows shot up. She was bold. "You trying to steal my necklace? It's a little rough for you. You don't look the skull and crossbones kind of girl."

"Oh, I'm all about poison." She leaned over and took the edge of my rectangular necklace into her mouth, giving it a bite before dropping it again. The metal fell against my chest. "And I like to use my teeth."

I stepped away from her. "So go find an apple."

"Asshole," she muttered.

Yep. That was me. Chloe was glaring at me when I turned. "What?" I asked.

She bit her lip and shook her head.

"She was flirting with me," I said. "And I got rid of her."

Chloe just shook her head again.

I made a sound of exasperation. How the fuck was this supposed to work? Look, I knew it wasn't her fault, but I couldn't read minds. I wasn't even sure I wanted to. "So what are we doing?" I asked. "I'll follow your lead since these are your friends."

Chloe looked around for a second. Then she tipped the beer in her hand back and drained it.

"Whoa, girl, no rush."

But she dropped the empty can and gave me a mischievous smile. Then she reached over to the sand, plucked an unused blanket up and took off running.

Not was I was expecting her to do. At all.

Since she was going in the complete opposite direction of everyone else and it was pitch fucking black outside with an ocean a few feet away, I jogged after her.

"Chloe! Where are you going?"

Several people glanced over at me with suspicious looks, like I'd sent Chloe tearing off into the night. I made a face back. What the fuck? I didn't ask to be there. I'd been invited. And Chloe was the one running for no apparent reason and I couldn't ask her because she couldn't tell me. She dropped to her knees on the sand and spread out the blanket. Then she rested on her elbows, sprawled out enticingly. At some point she had unzipped the hoodie so all of her flat belly was exposed.

I slowed down to a walk, glancing back to see how far we were from the bonfire. Everyone was still visible in the distance by the light of the flames and they were definitely loud, laughter and chatter reaching my ears. Dropping down beside Chloe I said, "Is there room on your blanket for me?"

She patted the flannel next to her and nodded. Typing on her phone she handed it to me.

*I wanted to be alone with you.*

That pleased me more than it should. "Then I guess coming to a bonfire was a bad idea, huh?" Setting her phone down on the blanket, I brushed her hair off her shoulder. "So what should we do now that we're alone? Any ideas?"

Chloe's eyes sparkled and she reached out and fingered the same necklace that Emily had just had between her teeth. Impulsively, I lifted it off over my head and put it over hers. "I don't want to smack you in the face with it."

When I kissed her.

That's what I meant. When I laid her down on the blanket and took her mouth with mine I didn't want to knock her teeth out with my metal skull.

She clasped it then rolled onto her side so she was more relaxed and was looking right at me. The moonlight splashed over her ivory skin. No tan, real or artificial, on Chloe. She had a little bit of color, the kind that came from just being outdoors in the summer, but there had clearly been no effort put into tanning. I liked the creamy milkiness of her flesh. I liked the upturn of her cute little nose and the dusting of light freckles across her cheeks.

Running my thumb over her bottom lip I murmured, "You're so gorgeous. But I'm sure you hear that all the time."

She shook her head.

"Then I'll just have to say it constantly." Leaning over her I kissed her cheek next to her ear. "You're gorgeous." Kissed her eyelid. "You're gorgeous." Kissed the corner of her mouth. "You're gorgeous."

Chloe shivered. Her hand settled on my waist and slid under my shirt. Using my left hand, I pulled it off over my head and let it drop in a ball on the blanket next to us. The hungry and curious look on her face did things to me, made my control waver. But I lay there for a minute, watching her expression as she explored my chest with her small hands. She traced the patterns of my tattoos and moved her finger along the outlines of my muscles. A few years ago I'd had the six pack abs. Now they were less defined and I regretted my laziness. But Chloe seemed to appreciate my body and we both jerked a little when she stroked down over my shorts and found my cock. I wasn't sure if it was intentional or not, but I was hard and she was very much aware of that now, if she hadn't been before.

Her breath caught. I covered her hand with mine and stopped whatever it was she thought she was going to do. "You can check that out later." I pushed her onto her back and moved one hand to either side of her shoulders so that I was over her, invading her space. She blinked up at me, fingering my necklace dangling between her small breasts. "You're gorgeous."

Then I kissed her and it was the sweetest, sexiest kiss I'd had in a long ass time. She twined her hands around my neck, strained up towards me, her mouth eager and moist and silken beneath mine. We kissed again and again, her lips falling open as I teased at her with my tongue and I wanted this, all of it, but more. I wanted the moment to go on and on, never end, that delicious oblivion, the ocean waves crashing over the shore below us, her soft sounds of passion arousing as hell. But I wanted more too, and I cupped her tit, teasing her nipple between my fingers. She arched her back into my touch in approval.

Her leg shifted to cover my thigh so that she drew our bodies tight together and I could feel the heat between her legs and my mouth watered as I kissed her deeper, harder, stroking my tongue over hers. "What are we doing?" I asked, my roaming hand finding her ass and gripping that tightness I'd been fascinated with since I'd first seen her walk away from me. "This is dangerous."

The thing about random hook ups was when you started drunkenly making out with a total stranger, there was an assumption of sex. Kissing led to sex. No stopping. No making out just to make out. No teasing extensive dating period where you got there slowly. You skipped all the bases and just drove it home. It was a shift in mentality, totally different from high school and early college, where I had been content to kiss and grope and get there whenever. But I was going back to Orono and yet Chloe wasn't a random hook up. This wasn't just getting each other off. But it wasn't dating either.

I didn't know what it was.

I didn't know how far she wanted to take this.

Her response was to untie her bikini top at the nape of her neck so that it fell slack, exposing the majority of her breasts. I guess we were doing that. I still didn't know what that meant, exactly, but I wasn't noble enough to be able to resist pulling those tight nipples into my mouth. It was like sucking on a berry, and I had the deep, base satisfaction of hearing her moan low in the back of her throat. Her shorts were so tight I couldn't get inside them so I stroked her through the denim, her hips lifting to meet my touch.

I wanted her with a desperation I hadn't felt in years and I untied the back of her bikini so I could rip it fully off of her. Then I tugged at her shorts, yanking them down. The bikini bottoms went with the shorts, a tangled mess that I couldn't get past her thighs. But that was enough to expose her fully to me and she shivered. Watching her face, I caressed her clitoris with the pad of my thumb and her head fell back in pleasure. When I dipped inside, she was hot and wet and ready for fingers, tongue, cock. Chloe wanted me as much as I wanted her.

I kissed her everywhere while I stroked inside her, teasing over her tits, her nipples, her neck, tasting her mouth, her skin, while I worked her delicate flesh with my finger. When she came, I only knew because she stiffened slightly and I felt the rush of moisture. But otherwise she made no sound. It was both satisfying and frustrating as hell.

When Chloe started undoing my shorts, I sat back for a second, breathing hard. I glanced back at the bonfire, aware that anyone could come strolling down onto the beach and see her naked. With my dick throbbing painfully, I swallowed hard, making sure I was shielding her from view of the partiers. She looked up at me in question.

"Is this what you want?" I asked. "Sex?"

She nodded. Then as if to prove her point, she bent over me, and pulled my junk out of my shorts. The first touch of her mouth on my skin made me groan, fingers burying into her hair. It was clear she wasn't skilled at giving head, and after a second, I pushed her off, holding her head between my hands. I needed her to understand what was happening. I needed to know she *knew*. "Chloe. What do you want?"

But I wasn't communicating any better than she was because her expression was one of confusion. "I need to hear you say it."

She shook her head.

"Shit. I'm sorry, that sounded so fucking rude." I kissed her softly. "Are you a virgin?"

She hesitated, but then she nodded.

Fuck. Fuck and fuck. I couldn't do this. We had had zero conversation about what this would mean, about what we were doing. I couldn't just bang her on the beach, her first time, without knowing what the hell she was thinking.

"We have to go," I said abruptly, yanking her shorts back up and into place. I crammed my dick into my shorts and zipped.

Her eyes were hurt and I felt a pang of guilt, but holy shit, this was just a big fat fucking no. This needed to not happen. With trembling fingers I reached behind her neck and tied her strings back together. Then did the same behind her back, forcing her to roll over. She just lay there, clothes all jacked up and stared at me.

"What? Don't look at me like that. We can't do this. I don't know what you want, or what you're expecting. I'm fucking leaving tomorrow, Chloe, and unless you can tell me what you're thinking I can't do this."

She started to reach for her phone to type me some kind of message and I exploded. It was pent up sexual frustration. But it was mostly the frustration that I wasn't sure I was even getting to know Chloe. It was like trying to date someone who only spoke Greek and I only spoke English. You can't hear anything about what's in their head. It's conjecture. It's assumption. It was me creating the sound of what I wanted or assumed her thoughts could or should be. It was like creating my own Chloe and that was fucked up.

Totally messed up.

So I grabbed the phone out of her hand and tossed it back down on the blanket. "No! Tell me what you're thinking."

It was an asshole thing to demand. I knew she wasn't staying silent on purpose but I was so frustrated the words just flew out. Her mouth opened, then closed again.

She looked away from me.

That deflated my anger. "I'm sorry." I drew a finger across her abdomen. "This isn't the way I want to do this. I want to get to know you better before we have sex. I can't just fuck you and leave you. It's not what I want. You deserve better than that."

Chloe sat up, still not looking at me and fixed her bikini top, making sure the cups covered her breasts. She grabbed her hoodie off the sand, shook it out, and pulled it back on, zipping it all the way up to her neck. Then she zipped her shorts and stood. I watched her silently, not sure what to say. Her jerky and angry motions spoke for her feelings. She yanked hard on the blanket I was still sitting on, forcing me to roll off of it onto the sand.

I stood up too, fishing my shirt off the ground. "Chloe…"

She held her hand up to stop me.

Typing on her phone she shoved it at me. *I want to go home.*

"Okay. Sure. Of course." I tried to touch her arm but she jerked away. "Don't be pissed. You would have regretted this," I told her, though honestly, I had no clue if that was true or not.

She gave me a scathing glare.

"Why are you pissed at me?" I asked, feeling irritated again.

Well. Maybe because I had insisted the girl who couldn't talk, talk.

She rolled her eyes and just started walking. I rubbed my jaw. I could smell the scent of her pussy on my fingers and I breathed deeply. I had pretty much totally fucked that up. On the drive home the silence was louder than it should have been given I'd gotten used to her not saying anything. But there were no smiles from Chloe, no laughter, no sparkling eyes. She stared out the window, her body language stiff.

I pulled to a stop in her driveway and touched her knee so she would turn and look at me. "See you tomorrow?"

She shook her head.

"I'm leaving at noon."

She just blinked at me, stern. Harsh.

"Were you using me to lose your virginity?" I asked, the idea suddenly popping into my head. Maybe she was just looking to get laid and I'd wrecked her plans.

Her mouth fell open. Then she just shoved the car door open and started to climb out.

"Hey, wait." I thought that was a no, but I wasn't entirely sure. "What the fuck is going on in your head?" I was being a dick again, but it was frustrating and infuriating. She had to understand that.

Chloe just slammed the door shut.

Totally pissed off, I brought my fist down hard on the steering wheel. It made the horn blare, and Chloe jumped. She shot a censorious look over her shoulder.

Fine. I reversed Aubrey's car and shot out of the driveway.

On the couch, shirt tugged off, I lay there hot and miserable. The air felt like it wasn't moving at all, and I had the memory of Chloe shattered beneath me haunting every thought. I watched the videos of her playing piano again, holding my phone up in front of me. At one point, the phone slipped and cracked me square in the nose when it dropped.

The video stopped.

The night went silent.

# *chapter*
# nine

*I* TEXTED CHLOE AND ASKED TO see her before I left. Her answer was simple.

*No.*

As I dropped my backpack onto the floor before heading out to the ferry, my sister gave me a hug and one of those long annoying looks.

"What?" I growled at her. I had barely slept the night before and I was cracked out exhausted. Frustrated.

"You're back to your charming self this morning. Late night?"

We were in the kitchen and she was making herself lunch. I was drinking the coffee that had still been sitting in the pot from her morning brew. It was lukewarm and bitter.

"If you're hungover I can make you eggs. They always help."

She didn't sound judgmental, but I was hyper-sensitive. "I didn't drink anything last night. I'm just in a bad mood."

Emma was on her hip and she held the baby while making a sandwich. She gave me an amused look over her shoulder. "Are you sad to leave your new girlfriend?"

Yeah. Some things never changed. Me and Aub would always take delight in giving each other crap. "We kind of had a fight." I chewed my fingernail.

"What kind of fight?"

"None of your business."

"I hope you're not pushing her to have sex or whatever. I think she's fairly innocent, Ethan."

I snorted. "We had the opposite problem, trust me. She wanted to bang on the beach and I said it was too soon."

Aubrey's eyebrows shot up. "For real? You were the voice of reason?"

That made me smile, just slightly. "I know, right? But the thing is, Aub, I don't know what she's thinking because she can't tell me. So I can't just nail her without being clear on what it is."

"So you just want to nail her and make sure she's knows it's just a hook up?"

"No. I don't want just a hook up with Chloe. She's different." I meant that. "But I don't want her thinking that we can have a relationship."

"Then how is that different from just a hook up?"

"It's more like a… I care about you but we can't date. But in the end, I couldn't do it anyway because even though I want her, I knew it would complicate the shit out of things and her feelings would probably be hurt. So I told her and now she's pissed at me." I knew it wasn't exactly logical. But I couldn't relegate Chloe to the same category as other girls I'd hooked up with. She was different. Very different. I *liked* her. But it wasn't like we could date, so what did I do with all of it? Not having sex was the right thing to do, I knew that. I just hadn't exactly gone about having the conversation in the best way possible.

"She's probably just embarrassed. She'll come around. Chloe isn't a grudge holder." Aubrey turned with a plate in her free hand and sat down opposite of me at the table. She put Emma into her lap, leaning against her stomach and picked up her sandwich one-handed.

"Do you want me to hold her so you can eat?" I asked. She didn't seem like she was struggling but it looked awkward.

"Sure." Aubrey passed the baby to me.

I sat Emma on the table facing me and watched her head loll around and drool drain out of the corner of her mouth. "When do babies learn to contain their drool?"

"I have no idea. When they're two?" Aubrey shot me a grin. "When are you going to learn to contain your drool?"

Funny. "I'm glad I got to see you. I won't wait months to come back again, I promise. It's kind of cool here on the island."

"It is. And the locals are charming." She raised her eyebrows up and down suggestively.

On that note, I figured it was time to go.

*C*HLOE WASN'T ANSWERING ANY OF my texts. After a half dozen, I gave up. Now I just sounded desperate and pathetic. She wasn't going to talk to me. So I went to work in a foul mood and when a customer offered to buy me a shot, I took it. Then I went out after work to the bar down the road and drank some more.

I flirted with a group of girls.

And I woke up the next day in bed with not one total stranger, but two.

My mouth was thick, my head was pounding, and I despised myself in that moment of initial awareness. So, what, Chloe rejected me and I did this? Was I that fucking weak? That determined to punish myself and anyone who might attempt to get close to me?

Reaching over a bare back for my phone, I saw I had a text from Chloe.

God. She had answered and while she was answering I was having a threesome I didn't remember. I rubbed my hand over my face. This was why Chloe deserved better than me. Even though I had wanted her in every inch of my body, I was glad I hadn't had sex with her.

*I'm sending you my thoughts.*

I frowned.

*What do you mean?*

She answered right away. It was ten in the morning, and the original text had been sent at midnight.

*Here. Doc share.*

I clicked on it. It was a document, several pages long. Maybe it was like a diary. Quickly, I closed it again. I didn't want to see it. I didn't want to read Chloe's thoughts when there were two naked girls bookending me. That was just wrong.

*Thanks, Chloe. I am looking forward to reading.*

The only way out of the bed without waking up either of them was to crawl down the middle to the bottom, under the sheet. As I slid down feet first, I got an interesting vista on the way down.

It was like I'd fallen into a prosthetics factory. Legs everywhere. Fucking ridiculous. I about broke my back bending my way off the bed and onto the floor but finally I was out, breathing hard, head pounding.

I found my jeans on the floor and I pulled them on. With phone and wallet still tucked into my pocket, I left. I hadn't seen my t-shirt and I didn't care. I just wanted out of there. The light searing into my eyes in an all too familiar way, I left the apartment building and got my bearings. I was about six blocks from my place. Shirtless, shoeless, and unshaven, I looked like I'd wandered outside in the middle of a heroin high. Keeping it classy. That was me.

In the blissful darkness of my apartment, I brewed coffee for myself, and flopped onto the couch. Despite my headache I wanted desperately to hear Chloe's thoughts. What was her voice like, when she had the freedom of many words instead of so very few?

I opened the document.

*My name is not Chloe.*

*Before she ran off and left us, my mother (adopted mother, not birth mother) liked to tell the story of how one day she found me staring in the mirror. I was about four, and I had pushed a chair over to stand on so I could see in the mirror above the fireplace. She asked me who I was looking at, amused at how intently I was staring. I told her I was looking at Ekaterina. Since that was my birth name, the name I'd had before they brought me to America and the agency told my mother a new name was a fresh start, it freaked her out. She called a shrink and told him to fix it. To fix me. Because she was sure I was becoming some sort of split personality or something.*

*It eventually became something she'd laugh about, tell friends at holiday parties, her hand petting my hair absently as I leaned against her. I leaned on her everywhere, all day, every chance I could get.*

*I don't remember that mirror incident. I don't remember seeing a shrink. Not then anyway.*

*But I do remember Ekaterina.*

*And this is her story.*

I stood up abruptly, and went for the coffee. Holy shit. Chloe hadn't been born with her name. I hadn't thought about that but it made sense. She would have been given a Russian name, and apparently Paul and his wife had changed it. Probably to allow her to fit in better in her new home.

But damn. She hadn't been six months old. What did that do to a kid?

Not good things. I pictured little Chloe, big eyes and a solemn stare talking to herself in the mirror. It got under my skin, I had to admit.

*When Ekaterina was still Ekaterina, she didn't need a mirror to see her own features. She merely had to look to her side and into the eyes of her twin to see what she looked like. That twin's name was Anya, and together they moved as one in the orphanage on the hill. The window looked down on the town, a bleak industrial city of squat gray houses and an equally gray sky. They never left the orphanage. They went into the yard, to play on the hard-packed dirt or in the winter the frozen ground and the slippery patches of ice that older kids broke up with their heels and crunched between their teeth or threw at each other or pretended to stab themselves in dramatic dying scenes.*

*But the twins were left alone to play together because they spoke the secret language of those who shared space before they were born. And they were happy in the way of children who are fed and have a roof over their heads and don't know any better. They weren't loved by anyone but each other, but neither were they mistreated. They simply... were.*

*Losing a twin has been described as losing a limb, but it's different than that. If a leg is cut off, you miss what it did for you, to learn to adjust your balance, you mourn the extension of yourself that is missing. But having a twin is like having the inside of you, your heart, your brain, interwoven with someone else's. You cannot open someone's chest, and slice out pieces of their heart and expect them to live. You can't take a saw to their skull, and unravel their brain matter like a knit sweater, leaving only frayed yarn bits in a lumpy ball behind. When you yank a portion of the sweater out, you destroy the weaving entirely.*

*So when Ekaterina was put on a bus, to an airport, and onto a plane that sounded and felt terrifying, and then into a taxi, in a land where no one spoke a language she could understand, the twins were unraveled. Everything was different. Everything smelled and tasted and sounded different and all the mirrors were gone. Ekaterina turned and there was no Anya. No comfort. No shared brain to process thoughts and feelings and to make decisions.*

*Ekaterina became Chloe who was sent to live on an island*

*with strangers who wanted her to speak their language.*

*But I could only speak the secret language of my twin, and Russian if you coaxed me. I learned English in that I could understand and could think it, and when I learned to speak it, I told my parents about my twin and they told me to hush. That I had no twin. The orphanage had never mentioned a twin. Why would they split up twins? They thought it was the mirror again, that I was looking for the other side of me, the Russian side, that my twin was in essence an imaginary friend I had made up to comfort me in my new strange world.*

*That she wasn't real.*

*That I didn't know what I was talking about.*

*In my head, I screamed for Anya, for the other piece of me that was gone, missing, removed with no thought to the damage it would create. I screamed out loud too and cried and begged and no one listened. So I took my thoughts inward, and I stole my words away from everyone. If they wouldn't listen to them, then I wouldn't speak, and they couldn't hear.*

*Eventually, I forgot how to speak.*

*No one hears my innermost thoughts, no one but Anya. I still speak to her, and that hole will never be healed without her. And if I see her again, will my voice return? I don't know. But I want to try. I need to try.*

*And I need you to help me, Ethan.*

*Help me find my sister. My mirror. My voice.*

My hand was shaking, and it wasn't from the hangover. I had asked to hear Chloe's voice and I'd gotten it. I could *hear* her. She was sharing something with me probably very few people knew-that she had a twin. And why she'd stopped speaking.

I believed her. Because while probably a lot of people would question Chloe and her memories, I didn't. Her sister wasn't an imaginary friend. You didn't create a sibling to survive an orphanage. Or did you? Maybe there really was no sister but she had convinced herself at three that there was. I didn't know. What mattered was Chloe believed it to be the truth and the undeniable reality that her adoption had yanked her out of a very narrow and scheduled world into one that was confusing and frightening.

It was clear Paul loved his adopted daughter. But how do you make it okay to a three year that they're surrounded by a language they don't understand? A smile is comforting but an explanation more so. It was why I hadn't been able to have sex with Chloe. I'd had no explanation. We all needed words.

The one word she'd known- her name- had been taken away from her.

I pictured Chloe as Ekaterina and it fit. She was so delicate and so was her birth name. I tried to imagine someone randomly changing my name and I couldn't wrap my head around it. Sure, people changed their name, took on nicknames or pen names or stage names. They gained and dropped last names with marriage. But that was a conscious choice. What had happened to her was totally without her understanding or her knowledge.

Totally unsure of what to say to Chloe, I stared at the text box on my phone and thought before typing.

*Ekaterina is a beautiful name. As beautiful as you.*

Then I added a second text.

*Of course I'll help you. Tell me what you need.*

# *meant* for *me*

If finding her sister brought her voice back, I'd do anything to see that happen. She deserved peace. Closure. If Aubrey had suddenly just disappeared when I was four it would have messed me up big time.

*Do you believe me?*

I paused, standing up to dig out some aspirin for my jacked up head. Was this a con? Was Chloe some sort of pathological liar? No. That didn't make sense. A liar wouldn't stop talking. Liars loved an audience. All they did was talk. Besides, Chloe had a sincerity in her eyes, her expression that I wasn't sure anyone would fake.

*Yes. I believe you.*

Maybe I wanted to believe her. Maybe I needed to believe in someone. Something. Maybe I needed to feel like I could help. Like somewhere under the selfish hedonist who was wasting his life, I still had vestiges of the guy who'd wanted to do the right thing. Who could be someone's hero.

She sent me a smiley.

*No one ever has ever believed me but I knew I could trust you.*

That meant more to me than she could ever possibly understand. I hadn't given her any reason to trust me or to find me worthy of her deepest, darkest secret. It felt like something tenuous but genuine was being established between us, maybe sprouting from my confessions about Caitlyn. I had exposed my thoughts to her and in return, she felt capable of doing the same.

*You can trust me. Btw, you should know that I really, really wanted you last night. But I didn't want to do the wrong thing.*

*You don't have to explain.*

I found aspirin in the kitchen and tore the lid off. I popped three into my mouth and then bent over the sink, turning the water on, and catching a stream into my open mouth. After swallowing and wiping my mouth, I answered Chloe.

*I don't have to do anything.* But I wanted to explain. *You're not just any girl.*

She wasn't. She was much more than that.

I didn't want to give her a chance to respond to that so I quickly typed again.

*What have you done to find your sister?*

*Just looked online. I couldn't find anything. I don't know what I'm doing.*

Hell, I didn't either, but I figured public records had to bring us some information.

*Tell me everything you know about Anya.*

Then I asked what was probably a weird ass question. But I asked it anyway.

*Do you want me to call you Chloe or Ekaterina?*

The pause was so long I wondered if I had ticked her off somehow. Or if she was unnerved by the question. Setting my phone down I dug in my fridge. There was basically nothing edible in it. I was craving a burger the size of Rhode Island.

My phone buzzed on the counter.

*I don't know yet.*

For some reason, I liked her answer.

# *chapter*
# ten

S O THE QUESTION WAS HOW did I find a girl that might not have the same name anymore? I had to assume adoption records were sealed since it was a foreign adoption. Chloe had given me almost nothing to go on. Just the name of the orphanage in Russia and the last name she and Anya had been born with- Volkov.

After taking a shower and washing the stench of vodka and guilt off of me, I picked up my phone to call my friend Kyle who I thought could help me. He was the kind of guy who could find anything online in one tenth the time it took anyone else. I had a text from one of the girls from the night before. At least, I had to assume that's who it was. She sent me a pouting emoji followed by a pic of the two of them naked in bed, one kissing the other's neck.

It said, "Lonely without you."

Delete.

You'd think I would remember something like that, but nope. Nothing. Which was fucking disturbing. The alcohol was really a bad choice. I'd maintained a whole three days of sobriety before blowing it but this time I was serious. No alcohol.

I called Kyle.

"Hey, asshole, where have you been?" was his greeting.

"Vinalhaven, visiting my sister, dickhead. What have you been up to besides jacking off?"

"Really, after jacking off, I don't have much time for anything else."

I snorted. "Hey, listen, how do I go about finding someone who was adopted from Russia seventeen years ago? I only have her birth name and birthday."

"That's seriously one of the most random things you've ever asked me."

"I like to keep our friendship spicy and interesting." It had been awhile since I'd talked to Kyle and I realized that I had missed having real friends. I'd been hanging out with acquaintances because I'd reached the point where all my college friends and fraternity brothers had been starting to give me a critical eye and concerned speeches. So I'd stopped talking to the majority of them, or at least had stopped hanging around with them.

"That is so creepy. Anyway, give me what you got and I'll see what I can do. Can I ask why?"

"I, uh, am involved with this girl, and this is her sister. They were both adopted from Russia and Chloe wants to find her sister. No big mystery."

"Russian twins? I'm in. Can I have the twin if I find her?"

"She's not a prize." I rolled my eyes and I scooped up a whole shit ton of dirty clothes off of my bedroom floor. I needed to do laundry. I needed to do a lot of things. But for the first time in about a hundred years I actually felt some ambition to make it all happen. Turning all my pockets inside out on my dirty jeans I found quarters, a bar napkin (no clue what that was about), a condom, and a lighter. Apparently I had been drunk smoking one night.

"Well, well, look who found his ethics again? Because you've been racking up the prizes for awhile now, my friend."

He had a point, but I didn't want to hear it. "Can we just focus on the issue at hand? Her birth name is Anya Volkov." I gave him their birthday and the general area Chloe thought she had been living in before being adopted.

"What is your girl's name? That might help me."

Your girl.

I liked the sound of that.

"Chloe Rush, born Ekaterina Volkov."

"That's a serious name change. It's weird, like one day you're one person and the next day they're like and now you're this, bitch. Deal."

It was weird. I didn't think that anyone had done Chloe any favors by changing her name. You couldn't strip someone's identity from them. "Agreed. But I think finding her sister will help."

I still couldn't imagine what it would have done if me if Aubrey had just been ripped out of my life when I was a kid. You didn't just get over that.

"I'll do what I can. And then you owe me."

"Sure."

Kyle asked me about law school and I evaded the question. I asked him about his girlfriend and he evaded the question. Then we were done and hung up.

Accumulating the rest of my laundry, including every towel I owned, I piled everything into a basket and shoved my feet in sandals. There was a washer and dryer in the basement of my apartment building so I headed down. While I was sitting there on the single chair, waiting for the wash to do its thing, so I could immediately transfer to the dryer, I opened another document Chloe sent me. I wished we could Skype, but there wouldn't be much point. It would be me talking and her just listening.

I liked that she wanted to share her thoughts with me. It meant a lot.

*This isn't a story. This is just me telling you what is in my head. I know that you got frustrated with me and I don't blame you. I wish that I could open my mouth and speak, but even when I want to nothing happens. My throat closes and the words are swallowed again.*

*But I like you, Ethan, and I don't want you to think that I'm doing it on purpose or that I'm using you to help me find my sister or to lose my virginity. I don't see being a virgin as something I need to get rid of, and me wanting to have sex the other night was impulsive, because you make me feel good. I feel sexy with you, not weird. I'm sorry if I made you feel uncomfortable. I'm sure you have a lot of girls in your life and I don't want to make assumptions.*

*I know that being around me makes it impossible to talk and do things in a way that is normal. I've met guys who either want to fix me or who think I'm going to be some kind of intentional submissive, and it's not that. I don't want to be submissive and I don't need to be fixed by someone else. I'm the only one who can find my voice and I guess, I just need to be accepted, the way my dad and my sister do. I feel like you accept me, but I frustrate you. That's okay. Just let me know if you can't and I will understand. Let me know if what you want is to just be friends, as much as you can be friends with a girl who doesn't talk.*

*But this isn't just about me. This is about you, Ethan. And how you don't like yourself very much.*

I stopped reading, went back upstairs for a glass of water, and swallowed hard. I glanced around my apartment. The blinds hadn't been opened in weeks. I never cleaned. There was a layer of dust and stickiness on the coffee table and the carpet was dingy and in need of vacuuming. When you slept all day you never noticed those things. When you moved around in the night, the dark, everything looked okay. You could fool yourself the way you couldn't in the harshness of the daylight.

Meeting Chloe was like being thrust into the daylight. It made me simultaneously want to tilt my head towards it and squeeze my eyes shut. I wanted to feel. But I couldn't look.

For several long minutes I sat there, doing nothing. I thought about the last two years. I thought about the next two years.

Then suddenly, I dug my sorry hungover ass up off the chair and I twisted the cord so the blinds opened. Light flooded the room, and all the dirt and neglect were brightly illuminated in the sunshine.

I texted Chloe.

*I don't want to be just friends.*

Chloe was right. I didn't like myself very much and I didn't want to live like this any more. My sister was right- at a certain point you had to jump off the fucking merry-go-round even if you landed in the dirt when you did.

My first instinct was to delete everything off my phone from every chick I'd fucked in the last two years. But that seemed pointless. I shouldn't try to erase the past or what I'd done and it wasn't even regret that I felt. Not exactly. We were all adults. We'd all done what we had wanted to do in that particular moment. Even if I was doing it to escape my own loneliness and fixation eighteen months ago on Caitlyn, last night on Chloe. I needed to learn to face my shit head on.

So no deleting. No erasing. It was what it was. I was what was. The question was, who was I going to be today?

I was going to be the guy who helped Chloe find out who she was.

That simple.

That night when I went to work I was polite to customers and I didn't drink.

And when I got home at three I lay in my bed and I watched Chloe on my phone and I fell asleep listening to her music.

I dreamed that she whispered in my ear, her hot breath tickling my flesh. I kept straining to hear what she was saying, but the words were music, not English. I kept turning to her to try and ask her what she meant, but she held my chin tightly in the grip of her delicate fingers. She had more strength than I could have ever imagined and I couldn't move without a struggle. The music swelled and surrounded me, boring into my eardrum like a power drill.

I woke up just as my head exploded.

A S HUMANS WE'RE HARDWIRED TO survive and buried deep in our DNA is the relentless desire to possess that which we can't have. It forces us to push through mental and physical limitations and survive, propagating the species. It's science, not stubbornness.

But the way it manifested itself in me during those weeks when Kyle was looking into Chloe's twin and I was staying sober, was to cause me to fixate on Chloe and how much I wanted her. I had gone from thinking she was cute but awkward that first day I'd met her to being unable to get her beautiful face, and her amazing body out of my mind. She ran through every one of my thoughts. From my coffee right after I crawled out of bed to my increasing need to hear her playing the piano before I fell asleep, she was there. In texts, in DMs, in pictures I insisted she send me. Chloe was no selfie-lover. Of the two pictures she consented to take and send she was self-conscious, shy, her hair falling in to her eyes.

Ironic, then that when I found myself finally ready to date, it was with a girl who lived on an island several hours away and who couldn't talk. Freud, and my mother, would have a fucking field day with that shit.

And the more I couldn't have access to her, the more I wanted her. I wanted to wrap myself in her hair and lose myself in her eyes. I wanted to drink her in, like vodka, and feel the burn of what she did to me all the way down my throat and through my limbs. I wanted to kiss her sweetly and I wanted to fuck her hard and most of all, I wanted to hear her say with her own voice, that she gave a shit about me and what I did.

I was falling for her and I wasn't sure if it was real or if it was lust or if it was chasing the rainbow. I thought I wanted it because I couldn't have it.

But when Kyle gave me the name and address of the twin, who was living in New York City, I knew it was my key to seeing Chloe. And I had to see her.

I had to know if what I felt was real, if reading her thoughts and hearing her music and 'talking' to her every day was the truth or a story I'd created.

My gut had me calling her via Facetime. I was kind of surprised she actually answered but my chest tightened when I saw her on the screen of my phone. She looked so... alive. So warm. The shirt she was wearing had slipped on her shoulder and I wanted to lick her skin.

Even as my dick swelled though I spoke softly, carefully. "Hey. I'm glad you answered. I have some news."

Her eyebrows rose up in question.

"I found your sister. Her name is still Anya. But she legally changed her last name to Strange two years ago. She's living in New York City."

Chloe's mouth dropped opened and formed an "O."

"She sings in a band, works as a cashier at a newsstand, and has a baby. I saw the pictures. I'll forward them to you." I hadn't intended to tell her all of that at once, but it came out in a rush. Like I wanted to impress her. Please her.

Or maybe I wasn't that self-centered. Maybe it was because I wanted her to be happy, to have her sister, but to understand right away that her sister seemed like a bit of a hot mess.

Tears filled Chloe's eyes. I thought they were happy tears but I wasn't sure.

"She's, uh, had a couple of arrests for theft and possession. Just so you know. It seems like she's had a tough life." I wasn't one to judge. Anya had been given up at birth and then from what Kyle had gleaned from public records, Anya's adoption had occurred six months after Chloe's but somehow eighteen months later she had been put in foster care.

Chloe reached up and wiped her eye with a knuckle.

"I can take you to meet her if you want. You should probably try to contact her first though, see if she is receptive to a reunion."

Anya looked like a bit of a hard ass. I'd seen a picture of her. Asymmetrical hair, lip ring, leather jacket, blood red lipstick. The resemblance to Chloe was small. I would never guess they were twins if I met Anya on the street.

Chloe bit her lip and nodded. She mouthed "thank you."

"You're welcome." My throat closed at the way she looked at me. Like I was brilliant. Like I'd done something really amazing. "Let me know when you want to make plans and go to New York, if you do at all."

She nodded. Then she looked away.

I waited. She still faced the wall, her hair covered her face so I couldn't see her expression.

"Should I let you go?" I asked.

Nod.

"Okay. Sure. I'm glad we found her, Chloe." For some reason, I kept feeling like I needed to warn her not to have high expectations. "Even if she might not want to meet you, at least you have proof she's real. No one can take that away from you."

She nodded.

Finally, she turned and looked at me out of one eye. I didn't know how to read her face. There was something there I didn't understand. But before I could ask, she waved and disconnected our call.

I tried not to be offended. There really wasn't any other way for her to end a call with me. But still. I wanted more. I just wanted more.

My phone buzzed in my hand.

*I want to go to NY as soon as you can. Tomorrow?*

No hesitation there then. Chloe wanted to go track down her sister in person. She wanted me to take her.

"I'm off work Monday to Wednesday," I typed. "We can go then. Can you wait two days?"

She responded immediately. *Yes. Thanks. Can you pick me up in Rockland? I'll take the ten o'clock ferry.*

"Of course. I'll be there."

I had no idea how we were going to drive to New York City and back in three days or how either one of us could afford a freaking hotel in the city but I had to be there for Chloe. I wanted to be the one there for her. I wanted her to look at me with hero worship, I could admit that. I used to have people view me with respect, admiration. Guys had wanted to be more like me, mothers had wanted their daughters to date me. I had taken that for granted, then I had eschewed it. I had thumbed my fucking nose at it.

Now I wanted to be neither noteworthy nor rebellious. I just wanted to be a decent human being, who took care of his.

# *meant* for *me*

And I wanted Chloe to be mine.

*The reason I did online dating was because it was an agreement between me and my dad. He never dates or goes out or does anything. It's him and the dog all the time hanging out on the couch. When Sarah and I kept giving him a hard time, Sarah even making him a profile, just waiting for his permission to make it live, he said he would only do it if I did it too. I was kind of surprised. Dads don't usually want their daughters dating, let alone online. But I realized that he worried about me the way I worried about him- he didn't want to see me spend the rest of my life alone.*

*Dad never talks about the woman who pretended to be our mother- let's call her by her first name. June. I don't like to call her Mom any more. A Mom, with the capital M, would not leave her children just because they weren't perfect, because I can say with utter certainty that no children are perfect. Just as no parents are perfect. That's not the expectation, simply the goal. So while I can't say I sit around and despise her, to me she is just June now. Not Mom. So when June left, Dad was depressed. Sarah and I felt guilty about that. I mean, if it wasn't for us he would still be with her. He wouldn't be sleeping alone.*

*But when Sarah said that out loud, because Sarah says everything out loud, Dad looked shocked. He told us he was sad because she'd left for our sake, not his. That truth be told, she probably would have left him years earlier if it wasn't for us. That she had stuck it out, trying to do the right thing, but that he wasn't enough for her. Never had been. She liked change, excitement. But he had loved her.*

*I think for me and Sarah, that conversation helped us let go,*

126

*move on. But Dad was still alone and I had no prospects for guys anywhere in my future. All the guys I went to high school with either were terrified of me (like I was some kind of modern day Carrie who might ignite their junk on fire) or they saw me as the puppy they occasionally wanted to pet.*

*So imagine dating profiles for a fifty year old man and a twenty-one year mute created by a thirteen year old. Sarah tried dramatic gestures first. Like Dad in the dark staring out at the sunset, with headlines she stole from The Fault In Our Stars. Mine was me in black and white, standing on the porch in my bathing suit, gripping the post, with "Take the road less traveled." I told her it looked like an ad for Maine tourism for pedophiles.*

*Next, she attempted whimsical. Dad was tossing a stick to the dog. For me, it was a picture from the summer when I was jumping on a trampoline at the fair. I'm not kidding. Trampoline jumping. I looked like a cheerleader on Vicodin. The headline was "I'll explain kerning to you." She tried a quirky About Me list for each of us, with things like "Loves chocolate! Hates mean people! A horror buff!" It was exclamation point heavy and more than a little manic.*

*What I discovered is that no one gives a shit what is on your profile. They look at your profile picture and they either keep swiping through their options or they pause and send a message that usually reads like one of the following: Ur hot. Wanna hook up? Hi.*

*I met a grand total of one guy from our little experiment. He talked to me like I was mentally handicapped then tried to get me to go down on him in his car.*

*My dad's profile was on a site Sarah deemed appropriate for an 'old person.' So his interaction with women was more* conversational. But they also all seemed to either want to hook up with him or get married on the second date. As Sarah put it, "Bitches be clingy." So what was the conclusion? That we all spend so much time playing the field, allowing ourselves to succumb to dating ADHD as a new profile popped up every two seconds, that we (the collective WE, not me) were never satisfied, until suddenly we realized we were alone. And then we wanted to skip all the dating parts and go straight for the Happily Ever After.

It doesn't seem natural. Organic. I wondered how all those Zoosk couples smiling in their "we met on Zoosk" ad pictures managed to cut through all the BS and make it to a natural, sustaining relationship?

Dad went out with three different women and came home shaking his head and rubbing his chest like he had heart burn.

Sarah was mad at us when we took the profiles down. She didn't think we gave it a fair shake. Some day I will retaliate and put a picture of her sucking a milkshake and use the headline "Shake It Up" for her dating profile the minute she turns twenty-one. But knowing Sarah, she will just talk a guy into dating her. She'll just wear him down until he can't resist and she has convinced him he's happy with her. Which he probably will be because no one will ever be able to claim Sarah plays head games. Everything she thinks comes out of her mouth.

One day when I find my voice again, I will open my mouth and everything I've ever thought will rush out like a verbal tsunami and I only hope it won't leave you knocked unconscious from the force, or sweep you totally away from me.

I was picking Chloe up in the morning and I lay in bed and

reread her words to me. I don't think she had any idea that she had already found her voice. It wasn't verbal, it was written.

It was bizarre to think that I'd missed her, but I had. I couldn't wait to touch her, to kiss her.

My room was dark but my apartment was clean. I'd spent the day dragging it back from the edge of disgusting to livable and I could smell the hint of lemon from the cleaner in the air. My window was open because we'd had a sudden dip in temperature and the breeze rattled the screen slightly.

I had been dodging anyone female for the last two weeks and I was hard, in desperate need of release. But I refused to jerk off. I wanted to strain the edges of my self-control. No alcohol. No women. No orgasm.

So I lay naked in the dark, thoughts racing around and around Chloe, cock hard and throbbing.

And I relished the control. The awareness. I felt ready.

Like Chloe had said, people seemed to have forgotten how to date. It was hook ups or forever. I wanted to give that to her- the middle ground. A guy who would do more than 'hang out.'

So I lay there and plotted my strategy.

# *chapter*
# eleven

*T*HERE WAS SOMETHING STEALTHY ABOUT showing up at the ferry dock but not having any intention of seeing my sister on Vinalhaven. I felt a little guilty and while I knew it would be more gentlemanly to pick Chloe up at her house, she hadn't wanted to waste time on me coming to the island and getting caught up in seeing people. Understanding she just wanted to see her sister, I agreed, but then felt like a douche sitting in the parking lot as the ferry pulled in.

Stepping out into the morning sunshine, I pulled the baseball hat I was wearing down lower. I was going for the any-other-guy look, an attempt to blend in and be anything other than noteworthy. I didn't want anyone to ask questions, here or in New York. This was Chloe's show, not mine. I was just glad to have a role, any role.

Chloe didn't act like we were on an undercover mission

though. She got off the ferry with a backpack around her shoulders and her face lit up when she saw me. I felt the smile spreading across my own face when I saw her. She moved so gracefully, shaking her hair out of her eyes, and I was a fucking sucker for her. I was ridiculously hot for her, but more important than that, I was falling head over ass in love with her.

I kept telling myself to fight it but then I kept not fighting it.

So I was pleased that she was pleased to see me and when she rushed forward to give me a hug, I opened up my arms and caught her, pulling her tight against me so I could feel her petite body in its entirety.

"Hi," I murmured.

Her response was to lift her mouth towards me, her head tilted, lips falling open. She wanted a kiss. I wasn't going to tell her no. If she didn't care who was watching, I wasn't going to give a shit either.

"Do you want a kiss?" I asked, lips so close to hers our breath intermingled.

She nodded.

"Okay." I brushed her lips with mine, just a brief, soft tease. "It's good to see you."

Chloe nodded again.

She clearly wanted another kiss, a deeper, hotter kiss, but I decided to torture us both a little. We had a long few days ahead of us and at some point during our trip I was going to give us both what we wanted. Me. Chloe. In bed together. Naked. The anticipation would be killer, in the best way possible.

"Are you ready? It's a long drive."

She nodded. She looked excited. Chloe's hand slipped into

mine, naturally, as we crossed the parking lot to my car. Once in the passenger seat, she unzipped her backpack and pulled out an envelope.

"What's this?"

Peeling it open, she showed me there was a stack of money in it. She put her head on her hands and mimicked sleep.

"For the hotel?"

She nodded.

"You don't have to pay for the hotel."

Now she nodded emphatically.

"Where did you get this from?" I asked.

Her arms cradled an imaginary baby.

"Oh, babysitting? Damn. That's a lot of diaper changes." There was five hundred dollars in the envelope. "I can split the bill with you. It's only fair."

She frowned like she thought that was dumb. Hell, maybe it was dumb. It wasn't my sister or my trip. But it wasn't like I wasn't going to gain something from it. I'd get to be with her. How lame ass whipped was that? Whatever. I wasn't going to let her pay for the whole bill. That would be just...wrong.

"Pick what music you want to listen to," I told her as I pulled out of the parking lot. Then because I hadn't touched her enough, I rested my hand on her knee and squeezed. Her skin was warm, smooth.

She put her hand over mine and laced her fingers over my knuckles. It felt natural. It felt right. Like everything I had done, everything I had missed, wasted, been waiting on, no longer mattered when I was sharing the same space as Chloe. There was something simple and straightforward and innocent about the way she cared about me. It was like she didn't fear rejection or care about impression, playing games, or being coy. For whatever reason, she liked me, and she wasn't afraid to show it.

Her musical choice surprised me.

"Country?" I asked, shooting her a grin. "And here I thought you'd be into hair metal." Which wasn't true, but somehow I'd pictured pure pop, not country.

She wrinkled her nose and pointed to me.

"Me? No, not hair metal. I like indie rock."

She rolled her eyes.

"What?" That amused me. "There is nothing hipster about indie music, you hater."

As we started south, I was surprised to hear Chloe hum a little. It wasn't humming in the truest sense, but it was a sound coming from her lips in tune with the music. Not words, but a beautiful sound that filled the warm car and made me relax, fall into the rhythm of driving. I didn't need to hear her talk, even if I wished she would. I no longer felt the urgent need to force her to speak the way I had when I'd met her. She spoke to me in her way- through music, through her writing. It was enough for me to feel like I knew Chloe. She wasn't the mysterious stranger speaking a language I didn't know any more.

Once Caitlyn had told me a story she'd read in a woman's magazine where an undergrad studying abroad in Italy had fallen in love with an Italian who didn't speak English. She didn't speak Italian. Yet after a week together, they'd made plans to marry and for her to permanently settle in Italy and I had told her I thought that was the stupidest thing I'd ever heard. She had thought it was romantic. To me, it had been wildly impractical and frankly reckless. How the hell could you know the other person wouldn't say something asinine once you did speak the same language? What if they were a moron? Or you had diametrically opposing views on life? Raging liberal versus ultra conservative?

Caitlyn had been annoyed with me.

But now I understood that we expressed ourselves in ways that weren't just spoken and that sometimes, the words became a camouflage for the truth.

So I settled into Chloe's silence and let her hum, and flip through her magazine while I drove the eight hours to New York. We stopped at a rest area and got lunch and she picked at her salad, though she did steal one of my fries. When I watched her trying to order what she wanted, I had a whole new appreciation for what it was like every day for Chloe and how easy it would be to settle into the life of a hermit. Since it was a fast food type restaurant, there was no menu she could point to in her hand. She had to hold her fingers up in the number of which item she wanted on the overhead menu.

The woman serving us stared blankly. "What?"

Chloe pointed to the menu then held up five fingers.

"I don't understand, ma'am," she said in a bored but irritated voice.

"She wants the number five meal," I spat out, equally irritated. How hard was that to figure out.

"Why didn't she just say so? Is she deaf or something?"

"No," I said. "And she's standing right here. She can hear you." It reminded me of when I had suggested to Aubrey that having Chloe as a babysitter was a bad idea and my sister had coldly informed me that Chloe wasn't an idiot. This cashier was making me equally defensive. Yet Chloe didn't seem to mind. I wasn't sure if she was just so used to it she didn't care or if she tuned it out.

"Look, we've got a line," the middle-aged woman told me. "What can I get you?"

So I had placed my order too and paid for our lunch that Chloe didn't eat. "Are you nervous or something?" I asked. "Or just not hungry?"

She typed on her phone. *Nervous. Maybe I should have warned Anya we're coming but I didn't want her to say no.*

"It is risky. But I understand why you want the element of surprise. She might not remember you though. Be prepared for that."

She gave me the look that indicated she didn't believe for a minute her sister wouldn't remember her. Hell, maybe she was right. But then again, maybe Anya's traumatic upbringing had messed up her memories. Or she thought Ekaterina was an imaginary friend she'd had. Who knew? I didn't want Chloe to be disappointed but I had a feeling she was going to be. Anya didn't look like the kind of chick who was all about the warm and fuzzy.

"Have you ever been to New York?" That thought had never actually occurred to me. I had been a number of times with my parents and once in college with some friends but I got the impression Chloe didn't leave Vinalhaven very often.

She shook her head.

"It's crowded."

She made a face like I was insulting her. Okay, so that was a stupid thing to say. "I guess that's obvious, huh?"

Typing rapidly, she then pushed her phone over to me. *Eight million people sounds crowded, yes.*

"I hope this hotel is okay. It's the only one I could find that wasn't ridiculously expensive."

Chloe reached across the table and squeezed my hand. She smiled and mouthed, "Thank you."

"You're welcome." My chest felt tight. "Now eat your lunch or I'm going to worry about you."

She was less restless the rest of the drive, even dozing off at one point like she hadn't slept well the night before. She had offered to drive, but I had refused. It wasn't that far and I didn't want her to stress at all about anything. Somehow I had it in my head that Chloe was fragile. I knew it wasn't true, but I couldn't shake the idea that I needed to protect her.

Which was really ironic given that I didn't know what the hell I was doing with my own life. I had pulled over for gas when I got the email from my advisor that there was no way I could start classes this semester. He said spring semester was a possibility if someone dropped out before December. Fabulous. I stood there inhaling gas fumes and fuming at myself. It was my own fault. I couldn't ask for any special favors. I had no right to anything other than what I had earned and this was what I'd done to myself. Didn't make me any less pissed off that when I decided to dig myself out of my hole I didn't have a fucking shovel.

I slammed the door too hard. Chloe woke up.

Her eyebrows raised in question.

"It's nothing," I told her.

Traffic was ass going into the city. I-95 South was crowded from New Haven all the way to the George Washington bridge and I was hot and running out of patience. Chloe made a sound in the back of her throat as we drove into Manhattan and I glanced at her. She was craning her neck in all directions to see everything. When she saw me watching her, she grinned. I guess New York City was impressive the first time you see it. For me, it was currently requiring all my concentration to maneuver the streets. The only method of survival driving was to gun it as every light turned green and then slam on your brakes at red ones. If you didn't move someone would honk at you, cut you off, flip you off, hit you.

After ten minutes of weaving, Chloe was gripping her dashboard and looking a little car sick, the smile gone.

The hotel was not the kind of place that had a doorman or valet parking. It looked like a hovel where only international students, hookers, and drug users would hang out. After parking the car for a price that made my eyes hurt, I carried Chloe's bag and opened the door for her. Yeah. My first impression was correct. The lobby was dark and dingy. The desk clerk was unmotivated and unsmiling. There was no elevator and if there had been, I wouldn't have used it. After hiking up three flights of stairs in a hallway that showed no hint of air conditioning, I was sweating and Chloe was looking worried. The bathroom was a shared one in the hallway and our room was filthy and the size of a rabbit cage. A yank back on the comforter showed dingy sheets and a stain of an origin I didn't want to contemplate.

"This is disgusting," I said. "There is no way we're staying here."

But Chloe just shook her head.

*Doesn't matter. Let's go see Anya.*

I glanced around reluctantly. "I really think we should try to find a new hotel first. I don't want you sleeping on this bed and I don't think I trust your safety in the bathroom. There is definitely a reason for the price point on this hotel and I don't think I can stomach a night here." By myself, I would probably tolerate it. Especially if I were drinking. I'd have slept in anything when I was loaded, which was evidenced by some of the places I'd woken up. But Chloe deserved better. "Your father would kill me if he knew I brought you to a place like this."

Her eyes flickered and she glanced away.

Wait a minute. "Chloe. You did tell your dad what we're doing, right?"

She bit her lip then shook her head.

"Oh, my God, seriously? Did you even tell him you're leaving?" Paul was going to have a heart attack. And hell, who could blame him?

She made like she was writing a note.

"You left him a note. Jesus. Does he know you're with me?"

She shook her head.

"You need to text him."

Chloe made a question mark in the air.

"Tell him that you're okay! He must be shitting his pants thinking you're in New York by yourself."

She just shrugged and made some kind of hand gesture I didn't understand before leaving the room. Okay. I had to assume she was going to the bathroom because I didn't think she was going to ditch me and take the subway to her sister's apartment solo. My head was starting to pound behind my eyes. I wanted to call Paul and talk to him but I didn't have his number. When Chloe came back I'd ask her for it. There was no way I wanted the guy to be worried about her or thinking that I was some evil predator who had stolen his daughter away. I already suspected the desk clerk thought I was involved in the human trafficking of Chloe since she clearly didn't speak and I'd brought her to the shadiest dive in the East Village. The last thing in the world I wanted was for Chloe's father to think the same thing. Well, okay, he wasn't going to think I was abducting her, but he wouldn't think my motives pure of heart either.

I realized I planned to be around for awhile and I wanted Paul to like me. I wanted him to feel that he could entrust his daughter to me. That his threats and fears were unfounded. I wanted to be trustworthy again.

My skin was starting to crawl in the small room that had zero ventilation and I pulled up a subway map on my phone, figuring the sooner we found Anya the sooner I could convince Chloe we needed to find a different hotel. I wouldn't let a pet goat stay in this hotel. When Chloe came back she looked at me expectantly.

"You ready to do this?" I asked. "I can get us to Anya's apartment building."

She nodded. She looked determined, stoic. A little scared.

I checked the lock on the door three times, wondering if we should even be leaving our overnight bags in there. Not that mine contained anything of value. I had Chloe's money in my pocket. I doubted she had much in her backpack either, but the thought of someone picking through our stuff was unnerving. I realized I still had quite a bit of the suburban middle class kid in me. A dive bar in Orono wasn't exactly the same as a dive bar in New York City. I was out of my element here, but once we were back on the street I felt better. It was still broad daylight and we weren't in a bad neighborhood, just a bad hotel.

Anya's apartment building had seen better days though, I had to say. When we pressed the buzzer for the apartment marked Strange I wondered about the bumps and bruises that had led Anya here to the city. And how she was possibly raising a kid here by herself, unless she had a boyfriend. Kyle had said according to public records she wasn't married, but that didn't mean she wasn't living with the baby's father. I figured we'd find out the answer to all those questions and more as soon as she opened the door.

"What?" a sleepy and irritated female voice said through the intercom.

"Hi, this is Ethan Walsh and Ekaterina Volkov here to see Anya." It made the most sense to lead with Chloe's birth name, otherwise Anya would never open the door. Chloe squeezed my hand, hard.

There was a pause. "I have no idea who you are. Go away."

"Ekaterina is your sister, Anya." It was my assumption I was talking to her since it was her apartment so I decided to go for it. "Your twin sister from the orphanage back in Russia."

The intercom was silent. Silent so long that I pressed the buzzer again, painfully aware of how tense Chloe was next to me.

"Knock that shit off!" the woman snapped. "My kid is sleeping. And I don't have a twin, or a sister, so go away."

"But-

"Go away or I'm calling the cops." Her voice was cold, emotionless. Serious. She would call the cops, I had no doubt.

I turned to Chloe. "I think we should go. Rethink this."

She looked pale. Upset. But she nodded and turned.

Out on the sidewalk I looked at her, the heat rising up from the pavement in visible waves. It had been in the low seventies back in Maine, but here it was in the mid-eighties, no sign of fall any time soon. My shirt was sticking to my back and Chloe looked tired, wilted.

I couldn't stand the way her shoulders slumped. Taking her hand, I narrowed my eyes as I glanced back at the apartment building. "You can't blame her. She has every right to be suspicious. So we'll just move on to Plan B."

It was a murky plan, but I put all the confidence into my voice that I had during my years of college politics. If you believe, they believe.

The hope on her face momentarily rattled me. Then I was just more determined than ever. "Let's be tourists for a couple of hours. Then we're going to watch Anya sing in her band tonight."

Plan B was simply this- if Anya saw her sister face-to-face she wouldn't be able to turn her back on Chloe.

In the meantime, I was taking Chloe on a carriage ride because when I dug deep, hidden under a layer of dust thick enough to grow potatoes in, I was a romantic guy. Chloe deserved to see that side of me as much as I wanted to show her. "Let's go to the park."

But before I could take a step, Chloe put her arms around my neck. She gave me a quick kiss, then a hard, shaky hug. "Hey, it will be okay," I murmured in her ear.

A glance behind Chloe showed that the curtain of the third floor apartment was pulled back. Anya was watching us.

# *chapter*
# twelve

I BOUGHT CHLOE A SNOW CONE from a gelato shop. We didn't go all the way to Central Park but to the much closer Washington Square Park and sat in front of the fountain. There were people walking dogs, jogging by, kids sticking their hands in the water. Tourists with cameras snapping pictures in front of the giant white arch. Chloe sat with her ankles crossed, mostly shaving ice off her snow cone with her spoon in careful rivulets like it was very important not to drop a single nugget of colored ice. Wanting to make it better for her, I sat there, wondering what to say. There wasn't any particular way I could fix anything for Chloe. It was coming up on dusk, the heat dissipating, and it had been a very long day. My shoulders were tense.

Watching her out of the corner of my eye, I marveled that I could read her so well. That I knew her so well. No one had so expressive a face as Chloe did. She told me everything with her eyes. Not specific word choices, obviously, but a general thought. I could anticipate her response just from looking at her and I understood her fairly obscure hand gestures.

"When do you graduate?" I asked her.

She glanced at me and held up one finger.

"The end of this year?"

She nodded.

"I can go back to law school next semester," I said. "I am seriously considering it."

Chloe squeezed my knee. I took that as encouragement.

"I'll have to move back to Portland, but it's no further from you than where I am now, just a different direction." I was dancing around the subject. So I decided to stop being a pussy and just throw it out there. "I want to spend more time with you. I don't want you online dating. I want you dating *me*."

Her spoon paused. Her eyes looked huge, soft.

Chloe was in love with me. I could see it. It was right there in those dark, limpid eyes. She thought I was a good guy and she wanted to be with me. Knowing that I had fucked up and that I'd made serious mistakes, she still wanted me. Not because she wanted to be seen with me, or she wanted my dick, but because she liked me. So simple. So innocent.

I'd been feeling about a thousand years old and Chloe made me want to remember what it was to be optimistic.

And hell, she did want my dick too, so that was a good thing. I was looking forward to that moment eventually. This trip wasn't the time but soon. After I convinced her to move to Portland with me and finish school there. She was doing it online, what difference did it make?

"Come to Portland with me in January," I said. "Between now and then I can come up and see you in Vinalhaven on my days off. But move to Portland so I can be with you."

What the hell, right? She'd say yes. I knew she would. She would be afraid to leave her family but she was in love with me and she would want to be with me as much as I wanted to be with her.

She wet her lips with the tip of her tongue. I reached out and touched the soft pad of her bottom lip. It was cool from the snow cone. "Yes or no?" I asked, voice low and rough. I was being impulsive, I knew that, but I didn't give a shit. I'd basically lived on impulse the last eighteen months and while those might have been stupid choices, this wasn't. This was me righting the chair I'd knocked over. Finding my way back to a life I was happy in.

Chloe nodded. Her lips formed the word 'yes.'

Triumph and satisfaction flooded me. "Good. It will be good. We'll be good. I promise you that."

I didn't know that. I didn't know anything. But I would have promised her the fucking Empire State Building in her backyard if I had thought that it would take that look off her face- that melancholy, longing ache for the sister who didn't or wouldn't remember her. She wanted to be wanted and I wanted to be needed. Relationships had started on less.

When I went to kiss her she lowered her snow cone so I could get in closer. I meant to kiss her gently but the minute my mouth touched her sweet, cold lips, I couldn't resist plunging my tongue in, taking her hard, forcefully. Mine. My Chloe. She was the first thing in forever I had cared about. Not just the first person, but the first anything. I wanted to be better for her sake. I wanted to be better because she was better and I wouldn't deserve her if I didn't get my shit together.

She even tasted sweet, and the tongue she couldn't use to speak did delicious and dirty things to mine. She was a fast learner and the initial awkwardness in our kissing was gone. I couldn't wait to see what else she could learn to do with that tongue.

The bench bounced beneath us and I glanced over to see some random guy had sat down on the end of the bench. Chloe gave me an amused smile. I guess in New York it really was impossible to get any sort of privacy. Our making out didn't stop us from having company.

"Later," I told her. "We can revisit that."

She nodded and her eyes promised me everything I could ever want.

CHLOE DIDN'T WANT DINNER SO I ate street meat off a cart. It was a decent burrito actually and even though I wished I could brush my teeth after I had a bit of a second wind when we headed to the club to watch Anya play. It was a nondescript bar/club that had graffiti on the bricks outside and a careless doorman. He eyed Chloe with naked curiosity.

"Do I know you?" he asked her.

She shook her head.

"You look really familiar."

Probably because she looked like the good twin to Anya's bad twin. Light and dark. But even though I'd only seen pictures of Anya, the family resemblance was obvious. Not identical twins.

But sisters. Chloe stepped closer to me like the bouncer made her nervous. He was big and tattooed as a doorman should be but he wasn't particularly threatening.

"She's never been to New York," I told him mildly. "So I doubt you've ever seen her before."

For a second he just looked at me, then he nodded. "Have fun."

"Thanks." We went inside, me leading Chloe by the hand. It was the typical dingy club vibe. Dark, the smell of liquor and sweat in the air. There were black lights strobing over the band on a small raised platform. The music was overwhelming, a crashing rage of sound that surrounded us. Not my kind of music at all. The crowd was eclectic but despite the fact that it was still warm outside, there was lots of leather. Or fake leather, anyway. But where there wasn't leather, there was usually bare skin.

Chloe stood out in sharp contrast, wearing a yellow sundress. No one there looked like they knew what the color of the sun was. It was black on gray on black. I felt comfortable there. I could pick out the individual scents of deodorant, men's cologne, women's perfume, rum, whiskey, vodka. People thought vodka didn't have a smell but I could pick it out of a drink at five feet. It was a cranberry juice heavy crowd. That and Sprite seemed to be the mixer of choice. The smells, the laughter, the drunken cacophony were all so familiar that I felt relaxed, at ease walking through the crowd. I found a spot at the edge of the bar and one lone free stool for Chloe to sit on.

"Drink?" I asked her, shouting in her ear so she could hear me over the band.

She shook her head, but she wasn't looking at me. She was

looking at her sister. Anya was on stage in a black bra and a very tiny skirt. She had the same shape as Chloe, but she had done something to push her chest up and out in a prominent way that shifted focus away from her naturally thin frame straight to her chest. They were definitely fraternal twins though. Anya's eyes and forehead were different, but she was beautiful. I wondered what she would look like without the heavy eye makeup I'd seen in every photo of her and that she was sporting again on stage.

I had been curious to hear her voice, to try to gauge if Chloe would sound the same, but her singing voice was more like a screaming voice and I couldn't tell anything really about her speaking voice. Her irritation through the intercom had been clear, her voice huskier than I had imagined. This voice was shrill. Neither of those seemed to suit Chloe. Anya definitely moved with a confidence and even a defiance that Chloe lacked.

"I'll be right back," I told Chloe, kissing the top of her head. She gave me an absent-minded nod.

This night required vodka. One drink wasn't going to kill me. I turned and gestured to the bartender. She was wearing tight high-waisted jeans and a crop top, a bottle opener tucked into her back pocket. I ordered a shot of Stoli and offered her one too. She gave me a frown.

"I'm not hitting on you," I told her. "I'm a bartender myself. Just offering a little professional courtesy."

Her shoulders relaxed. "Sure, what the hell?"

After she poured we saluted each other with our shot glasses and drank. The burn felt fantastic going down. It was a tight grip stretching my tongue down into my stomach, like a rubber band then letting it snap back. It shocked me into greater awareness. I paid her and went back to Chloe, limbs looser.

"You okay?" I asked.

She nodded. But she pulled her phone and typed on it and showed it to me.

*It's weird, seeing her. I've waited so long and here it is and it's just... weird.*

It was my turn to nod. "I know. She's a stranger. She's your sister but she's still a stranger." That had been my fear. That the four year old Anya was so removed from the adult Anya that Chloe would be disappointed. But she didn't look disappointed. She looked sad. Deeply, profoundly sad. Like in finding Anya, she realized she'd lost her a long time ago.

*I want to hug her. Just once. And I wanted her to speak.*

That made my chest tighten. I put my arm around her. "I know, baby," I repeated. "I know. Do you want to leave a note for her or something?"

She nodded. Taking a piece of paper out of her small purse, she set it on the bartop and scrawled on it. Then she folded it up and looked at me. I took a twenty out of my wallet.

"Give it to her in the tips bucket."

Chloe did, weaving through the crowd while I watched her from the bar. I noticed that Anya watched her carefully through narrowed eyes, even while she sang. Then she gestured to someone off stage to the left. I wasn't sure what it meant, but it became obvious when a guy in a club T-shirt accosted Chloe, taking her by the elbow and forcibly leading her off the dance floor. I moved forward.

"Hey! Get your fucking hands off her."

The bouncer glanced over at me. "I'm tossing her. She was

stealing tips."

"The hell she was." I wedged myself between him and Chloe. "We'll leave, but get your fucking hands off her right now." Anya had wanted Chloe thrown out. What a bitch. She knew full well Chloe was her sister. I was convinced of it. Otherwise she wouldn't know what Chloe looked like and she wouldn't give a shit if a chick in a yellow sundress dropped a twenty in the tip bucket.

When the guy didn't let go of Chloe I put my hand on his and removed his grip from her skin. "Back the fuck off."

Setting her behind me, I squared off with him.

"Look who's tough," he sneered. "Rich boy from Connecticut."

"Maine, actually," I said, smirking right back. I stared him down.

His gaze flickered to the right. We were causing a scene. "Just get her out of here," he said.

Chloe was typing on her phone. I took her hand and pulled her out of the club, making sure I kept an eye on the bouncer and the doorman. No one gave us any further hassle but I didn't relax until we were a block away. Chloe showed me her phone.

*Anya had me thrown out, didn't she?*

"Yes." There was no point in lying to her. She was smart enough to figure out that was what had happened. "Clearly she does actually remember otherwise she wouldn't have recognized you."

*Why?* She mouthed to me.

She looked heartbroken. Devastated. There were tears shining in her eyes she was valiantly trying to hold back. Damn it. My chest tightened.

I shook my head slowly. "I don't know, baby. Maybe it's just hard for her to dredge up the past. She wasn't adopted the way you were. She ended up in foster care."

We were only a few blocks from the hotel and the night air was cooler than the afternoon heat had been but it still smelled like the Village. Like rotting trash and a pervasive odor of cooked food wafting out from apartments and neighborhood restaurants. I loved the energy of New York. Hated the traffic and the smell in high summer. It might be September but it still smelled like August. Sweat and sweet and sour pork. There was a car honking somewhere behind us and a car alarm was going off. I hated that we were in public and Chloe was on the verge of losing it. I just wanted to hold her in private and comfort her.

Find the words that would make this right for her.

Not that any words could do that.

But I wanted to try.

But Chloe didn't look like she belonged in the City. She belonged in Maine, on the coast, the waves crashing behind her. On the beach on a blanket with me staring down into her trusting eyes. This environment only amplified her vulnerability. It put me on edge. I wanted to protect her, but I wasn't even sure from what, exactly. She wasn't walking fast enough and I realized I was half-dragging her. Taking a deep breath, I slowed my gait down to match hers.

When we reached the hotel we had to brush past a confrontation in the lobby between the desk clerk and a guy who looked like he was probably homeless and had wandered in. Up in our room, I made a decision. "Grab your stuff. We're not staying here."

She looked at me in question. I could see she was about to launch a protest.

"I don't mean leaving New York. Just this flea-bitten hotel. I can't stand the thought of you lying on these sheets."

Screw the cost. This wasn't going to happen. I did a quick search on my phone, found a hotel a few blocks away that had good guest reviews and hit call. "Yes, do you have any rooms available tonight?"

"Yes, we do."

"I'll take a king size please. I'll be there in less than ten minutes."

I gave the clerk my information and then I grabbed my bag and Chloe's. "Let's go. This hotel has a garage so we can drive there."

Chloe's eyes were still shiny, but at least she didn't look in imminent danger of crying. She looked bruised, though. Defeated. I didn't know how to fix that, how to make everything okay for her.

We had to drive past the club. Unfortunately, Anya was standing outside smoking, talking to the doorman. I thought Chloe was going to jump out of the car, but instead as she gestured for me to slow down, she rolled the window down and just stared.

Anya looked over and started, before recovering. She narrowed her eyes at Chloe, her arm coming up to hug across her body. With affected nonchalance, she lifted her cigarette to her mouth and took a deep drag. Chloe had dug in her backpack. She tossed something out the open window. I heard it hit the sidewalk. It sounded like a bag of coins or something.

"What was that?" I asked. Even though traffic was light, I still needed to pull away. "Do you need that back?" I'd have to find a place to park.

But Chloe shook her head without turning to look at me. As I hit the gas, I glanced in the rearview mirror. Anya had moved to pick up the tossed object. She stared after us. Chloe finally turned and settled back against her seat. Her shoulders slumped. I saw them start to shake as she cried silently.

Shit. I didn't know what to say. I wasn't sure there was anything I could say. So I just shut my mouth. If she needed me she would let me know. And I figured right then all I could do was just put my arms around her. I drove with one hand on her leg, caressing up and down in a way I hoped was reassuring.

The second hotel was about a hundred times better than the first, which it should be given the price. I handed over my credit card, figuring it was worth it. I'd deal with paying it later. I just wanted to get Chloe into a quiet room with a clean bed and let her talk or cry or whatever she needed to do.

But the more upscale nature of the hotel made the desk clerk look at us out of the corner of his eye as I checked in. Maybe we looked young. Chloe certainly did.

After he eyed Chloe for about the fifth time and was only polite at best to me, he finally asked her, "Are you okay? Do you need help?"

Considering that she still looked like she was about to cry, it was a fair question. She shook her head.

"Can I just hear you say that you're okay?" he asked, his voice gentle but firm.

I had to give the guy props. He wasn't about to let a guest beat the crap out of his girlfriend while he was at the desk.

"She doesn't speak English," I told him. "She's Russian."

Apparently the clerk was Russian too. Or at least Eastern European with a comprehension of Russian because he spoke again, and while my uneducated ear thought it was Russian, I wasn't exactly one hundred percent. I took a second look at his name tag. Ivan. Figured. Now Chloe wasn't going to answer and I was going to get arrested for domestic violence or some such shit when all I freaking wanted to do was give her some privacy and comfort in a clean room.

But to my complete and total shock Chloe answered him. In Russian. I couldn't understand, and it was only what sounded like a word or two, but she spoke. Out loud. She looked as stunned as I felt. Her voice was soft, melodic, very feminine. It was everything I would have expected her to sound like based on her laugh, and influenced in my mind by her music. She sounded like her piano playing- delicate, lyrical. There wasn't anything harsh about her speaking voice.

Whatever she had said reassured the clerk because he nodded and handed me the room keys.

"Room twelve-fourteen, elevators to your right. Enjoy your stay."

"Thanks." I put my hand on the small of her back and led Chloe in the direction indicated. We stopped in front of the bank of elevators and I pushed the button, my heart pounding heavily in my chest. I didn't know what to say. Where words had once come easily to me, now they seemed to stick in my throat. Hell, they didn't even form. My thoughts were erratic, even a little angry.

At Anya. At Chloe's biological and adopted mothers. At myself. Even at Chloe.

Finally as the doors dinged open I asked in a low voice, "What did you say to him?"

She touched my arm, forcing me to look at her. Ok, she mouthed.

"That you were okay?"

She nodded.

"Did…" I didn't know how to ask. "Did you mean to do that? Did it just happen?"

Chloe shrugged.

It wasn't fair that she could speak to the desk clerk and not to me. That was what I thinking, and it was selfish and childish and dickish. What, this was about me? But I couldn't help it. I wanted to hear her thoughts and she couldn't give them to me. But she could to the random guy behind the counter at the Lexington Hotel? What the fuck?

We went up in silence. I tried to shake it off. Let it go. This was about her. She'd seen her sister and after a seventeen year wait it hadn't exactly been a stellar reunion. So I took her hand. "What did you drop out the window?"

But Chloe just shook her head.

I sighed. I couldn't help it. It was an awesome thing to have feelings for a girl again. To look at someone and want the best for her and to want to know what you could do to make her life just a little bit easier. To feel that swell in your chest when you saw her and know that you could be made to be a better human being because you weren't all about you. But at the same time, it was frustrating and agonizing to love a girl like Chloe, who couldn't tell me anything. I could read her expressions, sure, but I wanted to share conversation with her, I wanted her to reassure me that if she could, she would.

I wanted to be important. To be the one that she confided in. The one she let into her secret world of Chloe thoughts.

Which was just me being selfish again.

On the twelfth floor I found our room and slid the card to unlock the door. Holding it open, I let Chloe pass. Following her in, I dumped our bags on the floor and gave a quick inspection. It was clean. Small, as most rooms in New York were, but it was definitely newer and stylish. I pulled back the sheets and found they were crisp white, recently washed. "Sorry about that other place," I said, sitting down with a sigh. There was a crick in my neck. I wanted a hot shower, but I knew sleep would elude me. I was too tense for sleep, and that vodka had only made me crave more.

When I turned around Chloe was right there behind me and she threw her arms around my neck. Before I even had a chance to react she was rubbing herself on me, hip to hip against me, and kissing me passionately. For a second, my body responded enthusiastically, but it was so out of character and so unexpected I couldn't roll with it. Setting her back slightly I searched her face.

"Chloe. What are you doing? Don't you want to talk about what happened?"

She shook her head and tried to kiss me again.

I hesitated. She had been on the verge of tears ten minutes earlier. This seemed like a bad time for our first night together. "I don't feel right about this. I feel like you're upset and this isn't smart for us to do this."

# *meant* for *me*

Chloe pouted. And put her hand squarely on my dick. She may not have subtlety or finesse on her side, but she had a raw and innocent determination that was appealing as hell. She wanted me and I wanted her and clearly I was a fucking moron to be hesitating. Yet I didn't want her to have regrets and I didn't want her to use sex as a way to ignore what had happened with Anya.

I grabbed her hand and yanked it away from me, studying her intently. "Is this what you want? Tell me."

She met my gaze, her dark eyes suddenly angry. I could see she was already reaching for her purse to pull out her phone for a lengthy answer. "No," I challenged her. "Just tell me."

It was asking her the impossible, and I softened my voice, realizing how what I had said sounded. I didn't want to further upset her. That wasn't my intention. It was the opposite of what I wanted. I put my hand on her cheek and cupped her soft skin. "Baby," I murmured. "I want to have you but not because you're hurting from seeing your sister. I want you because you want me and the sight of that bed makes you think of nothing but getting naked for me. So just tell me. However you can tell me."

Chloe went up on her tiptoes. She kissed my earlobe, making my shoulders tense. Then she whispered in my ear, the way I'd seen her do with Sarah. "Yes."

For a second I wasn't sure I'd actually heard her. It was so close to a sigh, a whisper, a haunting wish on my part, that if it wasn't for the shiver that rolled up my spine from her breath, I would have doubted my sanity. But then she repeated it. "Yes."

And there was no way I could possibly resist.

# chapter
# thirteen

"CHLOE," I MURMURED BACK, GRIPPING the back of her head, wanting her to understand how important she was to me, how her whisper had touched me. "That was the most amazing thing I've ever heard. A 'yes' from you is the most incredible word in the English language right now."

"Da," she said, her breath tickling the inside of my ear.

I smiled. Now she was showing off. Even I knew that meant yes in Russian. If she hadn't been pressed against my eardrum, it's doubtful I would have heard her, but I liked the intimacy of how close she was. I could smell her hair, her perfume. I could feel her hip brushing mine. She undoubtedly could feel my cock hardening against her thigh.

This time when her hands wrapped around me, I let her grip my shoulders and kissed the side of her neck. If we were going to do this, we were going to do it right. And I was in charge. Not her.

I was going to take her mind off everything but the way I could make her hot and wet and a whole lot of satisfied.

"Yeah? Well, if I do anything you don't like just say 'no' or 'nyet' or 'stop, motherfucker' or smack my head or put your hand up. Anything and I will stop whatever I'm doing. I want you to enjoy everything." I pulled the strap of her sundress down over her shoulder and kissed the exposed flesh. "Everything."

Chloe nodded and gripped my shoulders tightly. Goosebumps rose on her skin and she gave a soft sigh when my hands rose and I brushed both thumbs over the front of her dress, finding her nipples easily through the fabric. I remembered how easily she had come apart under my touch at the beach and I wanted to do that and then some. I wanted to make her come over and over until she had no trepidation and no uncertainty.

Stepping back a few inches I pulled my shirt over my head and tossed it onto our bags. Then I kissed Chloe, teasing with my tongue, reading her response, adjusting so that I was kissing her precisely the way she wanted to be kissed. I didn't adjust for me. Hell, no. She was meant for me. I kissed her the way she wanted so she could lose herself in the moment. In me.

As I deepened the kiss, I moved the other strap lower on her arm so that with a slight tug, her sundress fell to the floor. Chloe looked up at me from under her eyelashes and where I expected shyness I saw nothing but arousal. Hot, slumberous, aching arousal. The kind that only a woman feels, not a girl. I needed to remember Chloe was only innocent in the most narrow definition of the word.

Her eyes and her body told me what words could not. She wanted me to touch her.

It had been forever since I'd drawn out the anticipation of sex. Hell, even a kiss. It used to mean something, that moment where you studied a woman's eyes, her expression, her lips. Where you leaned in, then out, hovering, maybe undecided or maybe just drawing out that magic moment where you knew you were going to come together but you hadn't yet. Sometimes that space, that pause, could let you know exactly how much someone meant to you. If you wanted to linger, if you wanted to close your eyes and remember, they mattered. If you didn't, then maybe it wasn't worth it. Maybe there was no point.

With Chloe, I wanted the moment to last forever. The night to be endless. And our relationship to be infinite.

Her fingers softly moved over my chest as she traced my muscles. I did the same, caressing her shoulders, her arms, her waist. The swell of her breasts, the taut peak of her nipple. I kissed her neck, ran my lips down over her clavicle, peeled the cup of her bra down so I could press my mouth against her warm breast. She shivered and I stepped back.

"We need some music," I said, pulling my phone out of my pants. This wasn't just a get it on in the dark night. This was a thing. An event. A big fucking deal. I didn't exactly have a seduction playlist or anything but it had been a lifetime ago that I'd cared about shit like that. But I put it on the indie radio station on a low volume. Just something to fill the space.

Chloe raked her hand through her hair and pulled it back off her face. I wondered what it would feel like wrapped around my fingers, gripped in my fist. So I tried it. I tugged her head back so I could see her face fully, and her neck was exposed to me. She sucked in a breath.

"You taste so good," I murmured as I kissed her lips, pausing to see her reaction, before plunging my tongue into her open mouth.

We kissed on and on, like you did when you're sixteen and there was no hope of going beyond the make out. When the kiss in and of itself was satisfying enough, a hot wet display of intimacy, affection, of the special secret acknowledgment that you had crossed a line into something dirty. It was the triumph of knowing you meant enough to her that she was willing to go there with you. For you.

Then it had stopped meaning anything. It had stopped mattering. No one hesitated to cross that line and there was no point in staying in that space, that mouth on mouth indefinitely magic, where you got so hard you thought you couldn't walk and she was on the verge of orgasm from nothing but kisses.

But I wanted that with Chloe. I wanted to draw it out, to explore. To see how long we could go before pure desperation drove us to touch further. It made it less selfish, it felt like, to not just go for the hole in one.

Unhooking her bra in the back, I slid it down her arms, slowly, leisurely. When it was at her wrists, I pulled it off and tossed it onto the desk next to the lamp. I liked the way it looked there, splayed out by my phone. Then I turned and studied Chloe, registering her swollen lips, her pink cheeks, her glassy eyes. She was breathing hard, her chest rising and falling, her perfect raspberry colored nipples tight, goosebumps over her skin.

I palmed her breasts, and kissed the corners of her mouth in a way that made us both lean toward each other. She gripped my ass and stroked her way around to the front, where she found my hard cock. Her fingers went up and down on the length of it and I stepped back, ready to take my jeans off. I dropped them to the floor, kicked them away.

"Lie down, Chloe." I took her hand and led her to the edge of the bed.

While she climbed on, I found a condom in my wallet and put it on the nightstand for easy access. I didn't object when Chloe pulled the bed cover down and slipped under it, disappearing beneath a cloud of white down. Maybe she needed to not be so exposed or maybe she was cold in the air conditioning. Maybe like me, she was enjoying going slow, holding each other. Cuddling. For fuck's sake, I was looking forward to cuddling.

Whatever Chloe felt for me, I wondered if it was realistic. She hadn't seen the putrid rotting inside of me, the parts that I wanted to cut away, like the wormy bits of an apple, and toss aside. She saw what she wanted to see. Or so it seemed to me. And maybe what I saw wasn't truth either, because I didn't have the luxury of her private thoughts. But then again, how well did anyone ever know anyone else? Without benefit of mind reading, the miasma of thoughts that raced in and out of our heads all day long and even while we slept, were our own. We chose what we displayed or shared to and with others.

So I got into bed with Chloe and I told myself there was no feeling guilty because this was precisely what she wanted. She was an adult and this was her choice. I wasn't sure why my conscience was hounding me for the first time in years, but I told it to fuck off. Because I could see without her saying it, that Chloe cared about me.

"Have I told you that you're beautiful?" I asked, rolling onto my side so I could see her better.

She nodded, which made me laugh.

"Well, I'm going to say it again. You're beautiful." I cupped her cheek with my callused hand. Somewhere along the road of washing glasses and popping tops, I had gotten rougher hands than I'd had in school, and I felt it clearly against her smooth satin skin.

I kissed her and then I moved over her, taking my mouth down the length of her body. God, she felt amazing. Perfect. When I got to the waistband of her simple cotton panties, I left them in place, but kissed over the fabric, letting myself get a little more aggressive, eating at her sex, finding her clitoris and pulling it into my mouth with a sharp tug. The panties were a tease for both of us and she made soft sounds of distress and pleasure intermingled, her fingers reaching down to flutter over my shoulders. Her legs moved restlessly on the bed.

It was getting hot under the blanket so I nudged it back off of me and with aching slowness took down her panties. Then I eased her legs apart. Chloe stiffened and brought them back together, trapping my hands between her thighs.

"Do you want me to stop?" I asked, even though I was ninety-nine percent certain she didn't. It had just been instinctive. It reminded me of her inexperience and I felt a deep basic male pride that I was going to be the one to take her there first.

Chloe shook her head no. She took a deep breath and let her legs relax, fall open. She was the first girl in about forever who wasn't totally bare down there and for some reason that turned me on. Maybe because it meant she hadn't been prepping herself for dudes, maybe because it just suited her in that she marched to the beat of her own drum, or maybe it was because there was something free and unprocessed about it, like Chloe herself. Maybe most of all it said that Chloe did what she did because of Chloe, not because of anyone else.

Using both thumbs, I massaged her, opening her folds so I could kiss and lick her. I could feel her thighs trembling and at the first touch of my tongue, she jerked a little on the bed. I used my forearms to hold her firmly in place. "Relax," I murmured. "Let me taste you."

She was still stiff, but as I continued to slide my tongue over her sensitive flesh and suck gently at her clit, the harder she gripped my shoulders and the louder her breathing began. When I teased at her with my thumb, plunging it inside while my tongue swirled over her swollen clit, she made a sound deep in the back of her throat that felt like the purest form of satisfaction. I wanted her to come but at the same time I didn't want it arriving too soon so I pulled back and kissed the inside of her thighs, first right, then left. I drew her leg up and kissed the side of her knee and nuzzled her flesh down to her foot, drawing her big toe into my mouth. Chloe jerked it back and I relented, letting her have her moment of modesty or shock or whatever it was.

There was no foot fetish, I just wanted to feel every inch of her. Her movements were always so graceful and I felt that here too, even in her uncertainty and her inexperience. She had the body of a ballerina, but not the emaciation. She had more softness, heft. The long lean muscles with small but distinctive feminine curves. I came back to her inner thighs, but I just skimmed, flicking teasingly over her moist heat. My tongue dipped into her belly button. I took her nipple into my mouth, rolling the other with my fingers. I kissed her, so she could taste herself on my tongue.

And after I put on the condom, I teased my cock against her heat, running it over and over her clitoris so that she was squirming beneath me. Her cheeks and her upper chest were flushed with heat and arousal and her nails dug into the flesh of my back. She had opened her legs fully for me probably without even being aware that she had. I pressed in slightly, then pulled out again. I went a little deeper, until she tensed, then backed up, using my cock to rub over her hot clit again. I did it over and over, going a little deeper each time, letting her adjust to me, stretch, until I had sweat running down my back from the strain of holding back and she was clawing at me, begging with her eyes for completion.

Gritting my teeth, dick hard and desperate for her, I paused, brushing her hair back off her face, then without a word, I drove it home. Chloe gasped, and I saw her eyes widen with pain. But then as I paused, throbbing inside her, shocked myself at how tight and slick she felt, her shoulders relaxed and her mouth drifted open. I started to move, slowly, drawing halfway out, then sliding snugly inside her. Chloe looked mystified, restless, her eyes locking with mine than darting away. I knew what she wanted. An orgasm. I was going to give her one. Drawing her leg up and wrapping it around my thigh, I stroked in and out of her as I teased against her clit.

I felt her orgasm building, rising, her already tight pussy squeezing my cock so that it took everything I had not to explode inside her, to wait for her to get hers first. She reached for it, straining, her back arching, her legs squeezing, her hands gripping, her teeth biting. She wanted it desperately and when I ground into her, a thumb skimming between our bodies to strum her clit, she broke. She came in a hot rush of moisture over my dick, her head snapping back, her air cutting off. I felt the actual tremors of her inner muscles massaging me and as soon as she sucked in a deep long breath and let out a cry I joined her. So much anticipation, so much warm skin and hot kisses and naked, mingling flesh.

There was no holding back. I let go and I let her see what she did to me as we locked eyes. She tried to look away, but I gripped her chin and held her, wanting her eyes if I couldn't have her words. I let her see what she meant to me in my own gaze as I came and she came and we came together. Came together. That was precisely what it was.

When we both stopped moving, settled into relaxed muscles and frantic gasps for air, I fell onto the bed and pulled Chloe onto my chest. I wanted to stay inside her, but I knew that would be too much for her. She would be sore if I hung around any longer than necessary. So with a sigh I shifted her by the waist so she was resting on my hip. For a second I clamped my eyelids shut, letting the endorphins wash over me, letting the emotion lap at the forefront. Only good things. Nothing but pleasure and caring and intimate, tender shit. No guilt. No regret. No frustration that I wasn't enough and she couldn't talk.

Here, right now, we were perfect.

"You okay?" I asked her.

She nodded and looked up at me and smiled.

That made me grin back at her. "That was fucking amazing."

Her breasts pushed against my chest and she raised her

head so she could kiss me softly. I closed my eyes, suddenly overwhelmed. It was the sweetest kiss I'd ever received and I wanted to savor, to hold on to the moment. When she pulled back, her thumb went over my bottom lip, a barely there brush of flesh on flesh. It made me fall in love with her. Right then. Right there. The look in her eye, the small satisfied smile, it was everything. She was everything.

"You make me a better man," I told her. "And I want to make you happy."

She made a sound. She leaned over my shoulder and pressed her lips against my ear. "You do."

It was still a whisper, but her voice was huskier this time. I shivered, I couldn't help it. God, she sounded sexy. She sounded Russian. She sounded like a woman who had discovered the pleasure of lying naked with a man. With me. There was no doubt in my mind she was happy with me. At least in that moment.

Determined not to let real life invade the sanctity of our hotel room, I stroked over her cute little ass and kissed the corner of her mouth. "Can I do that again?" I asked.

She nodded, an adorable little blush marching across her cheeks.

The willingness turned me on, but I figured it would be really selfish to go at her again so soon, so I kissed her temple. "Good. First thing in the morning then. You should sleep. It's been a long day."

Chloe yawned, proving my point. She also rolled off of me so I could get up and dispose of the condom. In the bathroom, I discovered a smear of blood on it and I felt my chest tighten again. This wasn't a mistake. It wouldn't be a mistake. Because there was no way to walk away from this or turn my back on this. I couldn't pretend to not remember what had happened, like I did with drunken hook ups. I had brief flashes of fucking those two girls just two nights before. A kiss there, a mouth on my dick there. Me pounding into the one while she ate the other. I could see it, even if it was hazy and numb.

But this would never be like that. This was sharp and clear and swollen with raw, genuine emotion. I felt a weird sense of worry, the understanding that I had done what couldn't be undone enormous. You didn't just brush this off, taking a girl's virginity, with a nonchalant grin and a snarky ass remark.

Not that I wanted to. I didn't want to undo this. But I didn't know how to move forward, how to respect the importance, the sincerity of that act of concession on Chloe's part. She had given in to me and now I had given in to her. Looking at myself in the mirror I saw a guy who didn't deserve Chloe or her trust but who was damn sure going to keep pulling his sorry ass up out of the dirt and do what was right. She'd stolen my cover, my bullshit attitude, my hard assed determination to not give a shit about anything or anyone. She had yanked down that shield I kept so high in front of me so I couldn't get hurt and she had forced me to face myself and my feelings.

But that wasn't fair. Chloe hadn't torn down anything. All she had done was look at me and trust and believe in me. I had let the wall fall down because I couldn't resist the tantalizing idea that I could fix what I'd broken.

So now I had to stand up and be the man she expected.

When I came back into the room Chloe was asleep. She had pulled the covers up to her chest and she was in an easy slumber, breathing even. The light on the desk was still on, the music still playing. The Beatles. The Two Of Us.

Damn, that got inside and squeezed hard.

I went to turn the light off and saw Chloe's phone was lit up. It was just instinct to glance, not nosiness or real curiosity.

But when I saw made me pause and glance back at her again. She didn't stir. There on her home screen were three texts.

All from the same phone, which wasn't identified by name.

*Leave me alone.*

*Go fuck yourself.*

*I don't care if we were born sisters, you're not my sister.*

I deleted the last two. Chloe didn't need to see that. But I wanted her to have Anya's number. She must have left her number with whatever she had dropped on the sidewalk.

I thought about texting back but I didn't know what I could say to make Anya understand.

So instead I pulled my own phone out and texted Chloe.

Went for a soda. Be right back.

I put her phone on the nightstand next to her so she'd see it if she woke up. Then I got dressed as quietly and quickly as possible, shoved my wallet and the room key in my pocket and left.

# chapter
# fourteen

*I*T ONLY TOOK FIFTEEN MINUTES to get back to the club where Anya was playing. Singing. Screaming. Whatever you wanted to call it. I doubted they were done for the night and I was right. There were more people in the club than earlier but it still wasn't packed. I ordered another shot of vodka and I took it to the stage and offered it up to Anya, then set it at her feet, next to her mic stand. She gave me a look of disgust, but I noticed it didn't stop her from leaning down and taking the shot and drinking it in one quick swallow.

Positioning myself by the corner of the stage I leaned on a post and watched her. She moved nothing like Chloe. She sounded nothing like Chloe. If it weren't for the obvious facial similarities it would be easy to say that they weren't related. But I guess that was nature vs. nuture. Split up, they became totally different people, not the mirror that Chloe had said she looked into.

When the band took a set break Anya saved me the trouble of walking up to her. She came straight over to me and stuck her finger in my face. "Look. I don't know what the fuck you want, but if you don't leave I'm calling the cops."

"And telling them what?" I asked mildly. "I have just as much right to be here as you."

She frowned. "What do you want? Where is… she?"

"She's in bed, sleeping. Exhausted. We came here from Maine today just so she could see you."

Anya's eyes flickered, but her jaw was set. She moved restlessly, bending over to pull a pack of cigarettes out of her boot. "Well, that's not my fault. She shouldn't have bothered to look for me."

I was starting to think she was right. "I'm back because I saw the texts you sent to Chloe and I just wanted to tell you that there is no fucking reason you need to be such a bitch. Her intentions are pure here. She wanted to find her sister, that's all."

"I thought her name was Ekaterina." She chewed on her fingernail.

I wondered what she would look like without the heavy eye makeup. Probably a hell of a lot like Chloe. It was unnerving. So similar, yet so different.

"Her adopted parents changed her name. They probably shouldn't have, but they thought they were doing the right thing."

"At least they kept her. More than I can say for my alleged 'forever family.'" Anya made air quotes as she spoke. "Assholes."

"They definitely sound like it. I don't understand why they would do that to you." There must have been too much of the pity I genuinely felt in my voice.

She gave me a sharp look. "So why don't you mind your own business? Can't Ekaterina or Chloe or whatever the fuck her name is speak for herself?"

"No," I said flatly. "She can't. She hasn't spoken since she was seven years old."

Her eyebrows shot up. "That's messed up. What do you mean, she doesn't talk?"

"She has selective mutism. Look it up." It wasn't my job to explain it to her. "I think she thought maybe if she saw you, she'd be able to speak again. At least in Russian. I also think she just wants you in her life and she wanted a chance to communicate that to you."

Anya was silent for a minute. "I'm going outside for a cigarette. And I don't want you following me. Tell Chloe I'm sorry for being a bitch. I don't have any issue with her, it's just... I have a lot going on in my life and I can't deal with this. I just can't. It's nothing personal."

So that was that. "You can tell her yourself, either in person or in a text, but I'm not telling her that. This is between you and her."

She scoffed. "Right. Then what are you doing here?"

I couldn't argue with that. Pushing myself off the post I just turned to leave without another word.

Anya grabbed my arm. "Hey. Give her this back. Please?" She fished something out of her bra.

"What?" But I was already opening my palm and she dropped it into my hand. It was warm from her flesh and that made me mildly uncomfortable considering how much she looked like Chloe. Like Chloe playing the part of the Bad Twin.

The dissimilarities were unnerving.

It was a baby bracelet in my hand. Engraved on the silver charm was the name Anya in scrolling letters.

"Why did Chloe have this?" I asked.

But Anya just backed up, turned on the heel of her combat boot, and walked away.

For a minute, I watched her, expecting her to come back. To explain herself further. What person wasn't even remotely curious to learn about their long-lost sibling?

But she didn't. She wasn't.

When I got back to the hotel, Chloe was still asleep. Leaving the bracelet in the pocket of my jeans, I took them off and slid back into bed beside her. She sighed a little and turned toward me. Afraid she was going to open her eyes, smell the night air, the staleness of the club on me, I wrapped my arms around her and pulled her against my chest anyway.

She opened her eyes. That guileless trust in her eyes undid me.

I kissed her softly. She moaned a little when my hand slid down over her nipple, then her waist. That was all I needed to kick it into overdrive. I wanted her. I had to have her again, whether it was thoughtful or not. The day had been too crazy and I wanted to be there.

And maybe I wanted reassurance myself.

Or most likely I had just had a taste of Chloe and now I wanted another. I was still a guy and she was naked. Deliciously, warmly, wet and naked.

Gripping her ass, I yanked her leg over my hip, my hard-on immediately present and pushing against her.

"Can I?" I murmured in her ear, slipping a finger between her thighs. She was definitely wet. Either still wet from earlier or already anxious for my touch again. Either way I couldn't resist stroking her, enjoying the soft sleepy sigh of pleasure she gave me.

Chloe nodded.

"I need to get a condom."

She gripped my wrist as if to stop me.

"Are you on the pill?"

She nodded.

But then I thought about all the girls I'd hooked up with and how I thought I'd used a condom every time, but I couldn't exactly verify that and decided I had to suit up anyway. I hadn't been to the doctor and I couldn't take that chance with Chloe. "I'd feel better if I just used a condom."

Without waiting, I leaned over the side of the bed and felt around for my jeans. Digging in the pocket I pulled out my wallet and found a condom. I tore it open with my teeth and had it on before Chloe could change her mind or fall back asleep.

Lifting her leg over my hip I pushed inside her. She gave a gasp that was part pleasure, part surprise. Then I rolled onto my back and brought her with me. For a second she stared down at me, her mouth open, as she processed this new position. I lay there, holding her by the waist, just enjoying her warm body covering mine everywhere. My dick was ready to take action but I liked the sweet torture of not moving, of letting myself throb in her hot softness.

I could see the question in her eyes of what she should do, but I just lifted my head and kissed her. Surrounded by the waterfall of her hair on either side of me, it felt like I was in a private world of just me and Chloe. Never anything but me and Chloe. The connection was strong, flowing between us physically and emotionally.

"I feel very lucky to have you," I said.

In the curtain of her hair, our bodies joined, she whispered, "Me too."

It was beautiful. Because those were words of trust and love. I marveled at all the useless words I had said over the years, the lack of thought that went into them before they came out of my mouth. Chloe had a secret weapon. Her words mattered.

"I love you," I said, because there was no way to contain it. Not when she had been giving so much to me.

Her eyes widened.

Then because I didn't want her to say it back, because I wanted to let my words hang there, let her hold onto them, I lifted her hips and brought her back down onto me. "Like this."

Her head snapped up. A low moan came from the back of her throat. Then she tentatively took over, repeating my action. It only took a few times before she had it figured out and we were both breathing hard and squeezing onto each other. It took gritting my teeth and total concentration to not take over the rhythm, to let her take charge, but I did it.

My reward was she found her orgasm and it was gorgeous, big and full and all flushed cheeks and soft cries. I took over then, pumping hard up into her, loving the way her breasts slapped against my chest and her hair covered me. "Damn it, you're so fucking sexy."

I was being rough, but I couldn't stop myself. I could only

control myself so long and I was lost in her, in her beauty, her heart, her body.

When I came, I didn't think about myself. I only thought about her.

It was better than I could have ever guessed.

Better than I ever deserved.

WAKING UP WASN'T A LEISURELY untangling of warm limbs.

I jerked awake, Chloe shaking me hard. Eyes snapping open I realized she was out of bed and standing next to the bed, leaning over me. "What? What's wrong?"

Mind fuzzy from sleep, body still tired from the long drive, I tried to figure out why she looked so urgent. Angry.

Chloe dangled something in my face. My eyes crossed for a second before I realized she was holding the Anya bracelet over me. Shit. She'd found it before I'd had a chance to explain.

If I had been awake, I would have handled it better. But I said the first thing that came into my head. "What were you doing digging in my pockets?" Chloe didn't seem like she would go through my stuff. It wasn't meant to be an accusation but just a curious question because it seemed out of character. But it sounded wrong, totally wrong, and I knew it as I watched outrage cross her face.

She pointed to the floor.

I wasn't sure what that meant. Using my elbows, I tried to prop myself up so I wasn't talking up at her. I needed coffee and to clear my head. It took effort to interpret what she was trying to communicate. "I don't know what you mean."

Her lips pursed. She was already dressed in shorts and a T-shirt and she pulled her phone out of her pocket and typed.

*I found it on the floor next to your clothes. I stepped on it.*

"Oh. Sorry. I was going to tell you. Last night I saw you got texts from Anya and so after you were asleep I went to see her. She gave me the bracelet."

Her eyebrows shot up.

*You what???? You should have taken me with you!!!*

Uh-oh. I sat up even further, pushing the comforter off me. "I didn't want to wake you up. And I didn't want you to be hurt. Anya wasn't exactly friendly and I didn't want you to see that. I wanted to explain to her that you…" I stopped talking. None of that sounded right. It sounded like I thought she was a little kid who couldn't handle herself. I had been on the verge of saying that I was going to explain to Anya that Chloe didn't talk.

She figured that out, obviously. A sound of pure exasperation came out of her mouth and she made two fists. Then she picked up a pillow and hit me with it.

"Baby, calm down."

Because that is literally the two stupidest words you can ever say to a woman. Again, I blamed the grogginess.

Chloe hit me again, this time right in the face. Then she dropped the pillow, threw her hands up in the air, and turned away from me. She tucked the bracelet in her pocket, followed by her phone, then grabbed her backpack. Wait a minute. She was leaving.

No way.

I jumped out of bed naked and reached for her. "Chloe. What are you doing?"

Whirling, she held her hand out like she wanted something from me.

"What? What do you need, baby?" I took her hand.

She yanked it back out of my touch. For a brief second, she glanced down at my naked body and got flustered, her cheeks turning pink. Then she made a gesture in the air. A letter... a number. Something. Then she fanned herself. Did the 'sounds like' gesture then laughed.

What the fuck. What could possibly be funny right now?

After a second, it came to me. "Oh, money? You want your money? You can't be serious about leaving. Where are you going?"

She pointed up.

"Home? I'll drive you home if you want to go now. Whatever you want."

But she shook her head, pointed to me and made an X.

Nice. She wanted to go home but not with me. "Let me take you home and we can talk about it."

With a sound of annoyance, she bent over and yanked my jeans off the floor. In another second she had my wallet out and removed her money from it. She was serious. She was going to leave. Somehow she thought she was going to be able to get herself back to Maine from New York City with five hundred bucks and no ability to communicate.

"Stop. Just stop. Let me get dressed and we can hit the road." I reached for her and she dodged my touch and ran for the door.

Holy shit. I bolted after her but had to stop when I got to the open doorway. I was naked. She was tearing down the hallway and I doubled back to yank my clothes on and grab the room key so I didn't get locked out. By the time I got to the elevator she was already gone. I took it down, barefoot, and rushed through the lobby, looking left and right. There were two entrances to the hotel- one on Lexington and one on 42nd- so I had to guess which one she would have exited through. When I got to the street, there was no sign of her. I ran around the corner and still nothing. I even came back in through a Starbucks that was connected to the lobby and scoured the place for her. No Chloe.

Oh, my God.

I was terrified what would happen to her.

For five minutes I kept searching, then I went back for my phone and texted her.

She did at least answer.

*I'm fine. Just leave me alone. I'm mad at you.*

*Why can't we talk about this? I'm worried about you being by yourself.*

*And I'm sick of you thinking I'm a little kid. I don't need you to do things for me that I can do myself. It wasn't fair of you to go see Anya.*

She was right. I knew she was right. I did tend to act like she couldn't handle anything on her own. But it was different than it would be with another girl her age. She did have limitations. She couldn't deny that. And what was so wrong about worrying about her? It was a sign I cared. I'd always had her back. I had done nothing but offer to help her. I hadn't pushed her, in fact, I'd put the brakes on having sex on the beach. So how could she just walk out so easily and leave me to worry about her?

As I paced the hotel room back and forth, wondering what to do, I was both worried and annoyed. I wasn't known for having good responses to being hurt. I tended to lash out and hurt back.

Demanding the engagement ring back from Caitlyn was a classic example of that. So before stopping to think about how totally fucking stupid it was, I responded to Chloe.

*So what, taking off without talking to me isn't childish?*

Yep. Brilliant. When she didn't answer, I fought the urge to throw the phone across the room. Instead I took the used condom I had abandoned on the nightstand and took it to the bathroom and tossed it. Then I turned the shower on with no hot water. I stepped into the cold water and let it pelt against me with icy lashes both to focus my thoughts and to cool my anger.

It didn't work.

When my lips started to turn blue, I got back out and made a half-hearted effort to dry off before tossing my belongings in my bag and leaving. First stop, Grand Central Station to look for Chloe. Then Penn Station. Then LaGuardia. The odds of finding her were about nonexistent but I had to try. I also debated calling her father but I knew that would just worry him and there wasn't a whole lot he could do about it from Maine.

I was stepping on the subway when it occurred to me that maybe Chloe would go to Anya's. Cursing myself for not copying Anya's number, I decided showing up at her apartment was worth a shot.

As I held onto the pole and tried not to fall into the guy sitting in the seat behind me, I felt my phone vibrate.

*Childish? I can give you childish. I never want to see you again.*

I pursed my lips. Yep. That was childish.

Even knowing she'd done it on purpose, it still hurt. A violent lacerating, blood gushing wound of pure pain.

I'd fallen in love and our relationship was gone as quickly, and silently, ironically, as it had arrived.

# *chapter* fifteen

Y*OU'RE RIGHT. THAT IS CHILDISH. We need to talk about this.*

*Ethan. Stop trying to fix me when you can't even fix* YOU.

If she had tried to find the deepest way to hurt, she couldn't have found a better way than that. It was painfully true. She was right. I was a mess. A fuck up. Tenuous plans that I wasn't even sure I wanted to follow.

*I'm not trying to fix you.*

I honestly didn't think I was. Sure, I wanted her to talk, but that was fair.

*I care about you. I want you safe. You're making me sound like some kind of pervert who thinks of you as a little kid.*

The train jerked and I fell forward two feet. I hit send before I meant to.

So I typed again.

*I know you're an adult. But there is nothing wrong with me wanting to protect you and make things easier for you. If you're defensive about that, it's your problem, not mine.*

Yeah, that was the way to fix things between us. But it pissed me off. She was acting like she needed to put some kind of pedo alert on me. Yet at the same time she had been totally willing to have sex. So who was fucked up in the head here?

Truthfully, probably both of us.

Chloe didn't answer.

At Anya's, I rang the buzzer. Hard.

"What?"

"Is Chloe here?" I demanded.

"What the fuck is with you people? No. Go away." Her voice sounded trembling, like I'd woken her up or she was hungover or something.

I believed Anya. I didn't have any reason to believe she would protect Chloe if she were there. Standing on the sidewalk, backpack on my shoulder, I debated what to do.

The door to the building slammed open and Anya spilled out onto the sidewalk, a crying baby on her hip. An older guy had shoved her. He threw a diaper bag and a duffle bag after her.

"Hey!" I yelled. "What the hell are you doing? She has a baby for chrissake." Who shoved a woman with a baby?

Anya was wearing a ratty tank top, tiny denim shorts, and flip flops. Her makeup was running down her face, either from sleep or tears or both. The baby on her hip was sobbing, obviously terrified, his blond hair sticking up and his face beet red. He was in a onesie, his plump fingers clinging to Anya's thin arm.

"Mind your own business," the guy told me with a thick New York accent. "I'm evicting this bitch." He shook Anya, making her rattle back and forth on the sidewalk.

"Get your *fucking* hands off of me!" Anya screamed at the man.

At least now I had a place to redirect the anger that was boiling up inside me. "Seriously, man, stop touching her," I said, in a cold voice. "Whatever issue you have with her, you have no right to put your hands on her."

"Hold Asher for a second," Anya said to me, lifting the baby toward me.

I took him instinctively, cuddling him close and murmuring reassuring shushes in his ear.

The minute her son was safe, Anya turned and whaled on the guy. She went at him like an alley cat, swatting and kicking and hissing. "Don't ever touch me again!" she screamed. "Fucking pervert."

The guy tried to block her blows, and he stumbled backwards. "Stop it, you crazy bitch. You should have just paid your goddamn rent."

"I *did.*"

"Hey, uh, Anya, just let it go," I said, glancing around nervously. The baby had calmed down and was clinging to me, his eyelashes damp with tears, clear liquid running out of his nose onto his lip. "You don't want the cops showing up."

Somehow I didn't think it would go in her favor if they did. She looked fierce and down on her luck and in my experience the older white guy usually won in situations like this, baby or not. Bending over, firm grip on the baby, I hauled her bag off the ground and put the strap over my shoulder. "Let's go."

She gave the guy one last clobber than grabbed her other bag and turned to me, breathing hard. "Fine."

I watched the landlord over my shoulder until we were a few feet away. I didn't want him following though I didn't see why he would. "I hope you feel good about throwing a mother into the street," I said, because I couldn't resist.

"Junkie whores shouldn't have children," he said, before retreating into his building.

"Dick," she said vehemently, tucking her hair behind her ears. "I'm not a junkie or a whore, just for the record. And I did pay my rent. I just can't prove it. And when I refused to suck him, he threw me out."

That was appalling. "Seriously? Wow. That's disgusting."

Her jaw worked. "Just another day, just another asshole. He's about nine hundred on the list of men who have tried to blackmail me with sex."

That was really damn disturbing. "I'm sorry. So do you have somewhere to go?" We were walking, but I wasn't sure where. I looked down at the baby. He needed a hat or something. The sun was beating on his round cheeks and he was squinting as he tried to look up at me.

"I have a friend who lives in Queens. I guess I'll go there."

"Do you have money for the subway?"

She shot me a dirty look. "I'm not that broke." Then she wiped under her eyes and begrudgingly said, "Okay, maybe I am."

Her sigh was heartfelt and I felt bad for her. It must be exhausting to try and be so badass all the time.

"So what is up with you and Chloe?" she asked. "Did you

lose her?"

My chest tightened. "We had a fight. She got pissed about me coming to see you last night."

"You didn't tell her?"

Anya shook her head. "Dude. Bad move."

"Tell me about it. But I didn't want you hurting her. She's really sweet and sensitive."

She snorted. "Unlike me, you mean. I'm the bitch who would hurt your fragile girlfriend."

"Something like that," I agreed, because what was the point in lying?

"I'll take my son back now, thanks." She held her hands out with a wry expression.

"Sure." I handed him over and watched her hug him close, kissing his forehead. "How much money do you have, seriously? I can't just leave you."

"It's not your problem."

"You're Chloe's sister and Asher is a baby. I would be a total asshole if I just got into my car and drove off."

She eyed me. "Holy crap, I almost believe you mean that."

"I do." I pulled Anya into a doorway to a shop that was closed, boarded up and graffitied. "Here." Digging into my backpack I glanced around to make sure no one was watching us, and I pressed the ring box I had forgotten to take out of my backpack into her hand. "Pawn this. Don't take less than fifteen hundred for it. It's worth five grand retail."

Her mouth dropped open as she flicked the box open. "You want me to take my sister's engagement ring?"

"No. It's not Chloe's. It's from my ex."

She hesitated. "What do you want in return for this?"

"Nothing." I could see why she would think that, but I really didn't. I just couldn't stand the thought of Chloe's twin wandering around the city homeless with a baby. In a way, it was helping Chloe too. She would want me to do the right thing. I knew her heart was huge and she would help Anya in any way she could if her sister would accept the help. "Just don't end up in a situation you can't get out of it."

"That's cryptic. Here I thought you were going to demand I make nice with my sister."

I shook my head. "Why would I blackmail you into doing that? If your interest isn't genuine, it will just hurt her more in the long run. But I know she wouldn't want anything bad to happen to you."

She didn't seem to know what to say. But the box went into her pocket, creating a bulge there against her narrow hip. She was definitely thinner than Chloe. "Thanks."

"You're welcome." I touched Asher's soft blond hair. "Where is his dad?"

"Dead. Heroin overdose."

Somehow that wasn't surprising.

"And before you go and ask, no, I don't use. I wanted him to get off that shit but you just don't walk away from heroin."

"I guess not." I took her other bag off my arm. "Can you carry all this yourself?"

"Yep. Everything I own, in two bags. I've learned how to travel light."

She could joke about it all she wanted, but it wasn't good and we both knew it. "Take care of yourself."

"Yeah. And Chloe will come around. You don't seem like a bad guy."

That made me smile. "I don't totally suck, I guess. But she could probably do better."

"Well, there are definitely worse guys than you." She adjusted the baby on her hip. He was playing with the ends of her hair. "And I'll think about talking to her. I promise. And thank you."

"Okay. See you around, Anya."

*I* DIDN'T KNOW WHAT ELSE TO do when I kept texting Chloe and she kept not answering. So I wandered around the city, taking the subway to Grand Central Station and going down to the dining concourse underground for some food. It was hot down there and crowded, hard to breathe, no air movement. It was like being caught in the armpit of a fat guy. I ordered a deli sandwich and muscled my way to a free table to sit down and eat it. Chloe finally texted me back.

*Taking the train to Portland. Dad is picking me up.*

Great. Now her father thought I'd abandoned her in New York.

Before I could respond she sent another message.

*When your phone was on the desk you got a picture from some girl named Lila of her vagina. I deleted it. I shouldn't have touched your phone, sorry.*

Well, that was just the last thing in the fucking world I needed right now.

*I haven't talked to Lila since I met you.*

That was the truth. I hadn't.

*I'm not sure it matters.*

*Everything matters.*

I tossed my pickle to the side of the wax wrapper and picked up my sandwich. It wasn't an unfamiliar feeling, not knowing what to do, but it frustrated me even more now than it ever had. I missed Chloe, as stupid as it sounded. I wanted to bury my lips in her hair and hold her in my arms. I wanted to hear the whisper of her voice in my ear and feel her fingers tentatively stroke across my chest. How could something so right go wrong so quickly?

*I miss you.*

Yep. I went there. Thereby confirming my status as the most pathetic asshole ever.

*Please don't. Not right now.*

*When?*

I mean, I'd already thrown it out there, so I might as well roll with it.

*I don't know. Maybe we both need to figure stuff out.*

My phone fell out of my hand. I bit my sandwich. What was there to say to that? Nothing. Figure what out? I could figure out how to stop drinking and what the fuck to do with my future and she could figure out how to talk.

If we waited for any of those to happen we might be waiting a long ass time. Part of me wanted to throw the night before in her face, but I restrained myself.

She beat me to it anyway.

*Last night was a mistake. I'm sorry.*

Just like that she reduced what was damn near a religious experience for me to a regret. In a text. She might as well have put a hashtag in front of it. #oops #lostmyvirginity #forgothisname

As dozens and dozens of people moved around me in the hot

cave under the main dome of the station, I flicked at my pickle with my finger and thought about why I was even in the city. I didn't even like New York that much and I sure in the hell didn't like driving sixteen hours round trip in three days to spend an insanely large amount of money on a hotel room. But I had done it without question because for weeks, even without the ability to see Chloe in person, I had been falling for her. The more I read her texts and messages and her personal stories she sent, the more I had listened to her piano playing, the more I had seen who she was, and it was beautiful. She was a beautiful person inside and out.

Maybe she didn't want me to be overprotective. Maybe she had spent her whole life having her father treat her that way.

That didn't mean that she could get mad about one little thing and just throw over our whole relationship.

There was no way that what we had done the night before was a mistake. I knew what mistakes were. I knew when I woke up and felt that pit in my gut and had that momentary hesitation where I tried to piece together what had happened the night before that I'd made a mistake, no matter what I'd done.

Sex with Chloe was no mistake.

I had made so many mistakes. Now I was done with mistakes.

She wanted me to fix myself? Sure. I could do that. But there was no reason that she and I couldn't communicate and fix what we needed to together.

The night before had been the total opposite of how I'd felt and viewed every sexual encounter in the last eighteen months. It had meant something. And I would be fucking damned if I was going to just roll over and let her relegate me to the status of Her

First with nothing more than a backward glance.

I stood up and tossed the rest of my lunch in the trash.

Then I went to get my car and drive to Rockport to take the ferry to Vinalhaven.

As I walked down the street I sent Chloe a text.

*Last night was no mistake. A mistake would be turning your back on the one guy who actually hears what you have to say.*

# chapter
## sixteen

*I*F THE MIRROR SHATTERS, DO *you still exist? If you can't look and see your reflection, how do you know you're still there? You can look down and see your arms, and see your legs, but what if your face isn't the same? You can't check, so do you really, truly know?*

*When I saw my sister for the first time, I expected to feel something more. Instead what I felt was the incongruous reality of staring at a stranger. I thought Anya would look more like me. Or I would look more like Anya. That despite all those years apart, somehow we would have mimicked each other's style and movements, without being consciously aware of it.*

*What I saw was a completely separate human being, whose expression revealed nothing. Which seemed especially startling because my expressions show everything. My face is my words. The tilt of my mouth, my forehead, those are my sentences.*

*So when I saw my sister and I saw nothing I felt as if the entire foundation on which I'd built my life crumbled out from under me.*

*Nothing makes sense, nothing is real or solid.*

*I think I love you, Ethan, but how do I know? And how do I know that what you love is me, versus what you think is me?*

*Without a twin, without a purpose, without the need to prove that my sister is real, what is left of me? Am I really just the weird silent girl that no mother wanted?*

*I don't know.*

*I don't know anything.*

*All I know is that I'm grateful to you.*

*But until I can speak I have nothing left to say.*

*I* WAS HALFWAY HOME WHEN *I* got the message from Chloe. And then I really got the message. She didn't want me. I had been, what? A distraction maybe? A fantasy? I wasn't sure.

But "I think I love you, but" wasn't what I needed or wanted to hear. Even I had a threshold for how pathetic I could be and I wasn't going to crawl my ass to Vinalhaven and beg. No, instead I was going to lie on my couch in the dark and listen to Chloe's piano playing on my phone. So much less pathetic.

My body was tired from the tumultuous two days and very little sleep, but my mind was racing as I kicked off my shoes and crawled onto the couch. I waited for my thoughts to sort themselves out, for a plan to formulate. I waited for the impulsive urge to go to the bar, to drink, to bury myself in a willing partner to surface, but it didn't. I wanted to be with Chloe or I wanted to be alone.

Maybe she didn't believe that what I felt was real or solid, but I knew that it was. I was twenty-five, not sixteen. I wasn't in the business of telling chicks that I was in love with them for no apparent reason.

I wondered what she had told her father about why we were in New York. The truth? I had no idea. She'd said her father didn't believe she had a twin. So it seemed unlikely that he would now. It wasn't like we had actual documents or DNA proof. So really, what was different in her life?

It pissed me off that she doubted my feelings. That was her shit, not mine. I hadn't wavered. And falling in love with her had reminded me exactly who I was. I was loyal. I was decent. I was someone who went after what I wanted and I got it, but not at the expense of other people. Until twenty-three I'd been a go-getter and now I had fallen into a pattern of rolling over and letting life just happen.

That wasn't me. It had made me incredibly unhappy.

Chloe had helped me hold that very mirror she talked about up to myself and see exactly who I had become- someone I didn't respect. Someone miserable. It wasn't me. It was me with a mask, a shield.

So you know what? I didn't need fixing. Nothing I had done with Chloe was wrong. And while I was sometimes frustrated with her, I'd never asked her to change either. I'd asked her to move in with me, not go to therapy or work on her disorder. I'd read all about those techniques they used, forcing mute people to speak if they wanted something and making them repeat to others what they said to those they were comfortable with. I figured that was her choice, her decision, not mine.

Fuck this noise.

I stood up. I was going to Vinalhaven. I was telling Chloe I'd seen Anya again because I didn't need that shit coming back to haunt me, when all I had been doing was looking for her. And then I was going to tell Chloe exactly what I thought of her avoidance techniques and lay on the line what I wanted.

Her.

I wanted her.

WHEN I HAD PROPOSED TO Caitlyn, I had gone the route of what social media encouraged us to do- The Grand Gesture. I had pulled out a ring at the top of the fraternity house stairs at the homecoming ball in front of a hundred people. It had never once occurred to me that she would say no, and she didn't. But now, two years later, I realized that some moments in life are meant to be private. Like a first kiss. The first "I love you." Arguments. Marriage proposals. It wasn't about finding the perfect way to Instagram personal milestones in life. It was about living them with the person who had your heart.

I could have waited days, weeks, months to see Chloe. I could have let her work through her disappointment with Anya and I could have enrolled in law school, found an apartment, handed her a key and a ring with a quartet behind me playing one of her favorite classical pieces and a honeymoon booked to Russia to see where she was born, or something like that. Balloons and flowers and a photographer hidden in the bushes. Even if I were sure of her response, which I wasn't, I wouldn't have done that.

With Chloe, everything was so raw, so genuine. This had to

stay that way too.

Just me and her.

W HEN I GOT TO VINALHAVEN my sister and Emma were waiting for me in the parking lot. Seeing Aubrey holding her baby, smiling at me, reminded me of Anya, and her being tossed out onto the street by her landlord. I had to admire what she was trying to do, raise a kid by herself. Neither she nor Chloe had had an easy life and where it had made Anya hard, it had made Chloe tender. She felt things so deeply that it had created her mutism.

But I honestly didn't see that as a flaw. It was something I loved about her- that she cared so much.

"You're nuts," was my sister's greeting.

"Probably."

"Paul was having a cow. He thought you and Chloe ran off and eloped or something."

"If we were eloping I would have stayed in Maine where you don't need a marriage license." I took Emma from Aubrey and held her up in front of me, giving her a kiss. "Hey kid. Your mom's a jerk, did you know that? Did you know that?"

Aubrey laughed. "It runs in the family. But seriously, I thought this had something to do with Caitlyn and Heath getting married last weekend."

I'd actually forgotten Caitlyn was getting married. "This has nothing to do with that," I said mildly. "Chloe asked me to help her look into her adoption, that's all. The rest is up to her to share. But I will say I don't think she got the answer she wanted."

We walked over to Aubrey's car and she unlocked it. "Can

you put Emma in her carseat?"

"I'll try. But you should inspect my work afterwards."

"Of course. So why are you here, Ethan? I know it's not because you missed me so much you had to come back."

"Chloe and I had a bit of an argument. I decided I wasn't going to let her go underground when we should talk about it."

"Does that mean she dumped you and you are trying to pretend she didn't?"

I made a face at my sister as I shut the door, Emma securely in her seat. "You know, for once, a little sympathy would be nice."

"I'm terrible at showing my emotions, you know. I like to turn everything into a snarky comment." Aubrey studied me. "You care about her a lot, don't you?"

I nodded. "I do. And this is different, Aub. I enjoy being with Chloe. I think about her in terms of what can I do to make her happy, not what she can do to make me happy."

"You know, the ironic thing is you've always been great at relationships. If anyone can commit to a girl and do it well, it's you. That's why I never understood this whole Jersey Shore thing you had going on. It wasn't a good fit."

"Thanks, I think." I went around to the passenger side of the car and got in. "Drop me off at Chloe's, will you?"

"Of course. I didn't want to cook dinner for you anyway."

That made me laugh. "You weren't going to cook. Give me a break."

"No. I totally wasn't."

195

# *meant* for *me*

A T CHLOE'S I KNOCKED ON the front door. Sarah opened it and her eyes widened. "Chloe!" she yelled over her shoulder. Then she shook her head at me. "You're lucky my dad doesn't shoot you. He literally almost died worrying about Chloe. I would have been an orphan. Again."

This was a promising start to this visit.

The dog ran out to greet me and I petted her head. At least someone seemed glad to see me.

Chloe appeared in the doorway and she didn't actually look surprised. Nor did she look pissed. But it wasn't exactly a warm welcome. She just raised her hand and waved to me.

"Hi. Can we talk?"

She nodded and shot Sarah a warning look.

"Do I have to go? Seriously? Nothing interesting ever happens around here and when it does, I can't watch."

Chloe pointed and Sarah went back into the house, shoulders slumped.

I sat down on the front porch steps and patted the spot next to me. She did sit down, but at least two feet away from me. I decided to do this her way. Pulling my phone out I started writing and when I was done I showed it to her.

*I went to Anya's looking for you. She was being evicted so I gave her some money. I wasn't trying to interfere but she's your sister and she's clearly struggling so I did what I thought was right. I want you to hear that from me, not her.*

She gave a slight nod, tucking her hair behind but she didn't give me a response.

I typed again.

*I don't want to fix you. I just want you. Exactly the way you*

196

*are. I don't say I love you easily. But I love you.*

She bit her lip as she read my words. Then she looked over at me and her luminous dark eyes were shining with tears. God, I loved her.

"I love you. I love you in a way that is deep and pure. Loving you reminds me of who I am, and loving you isn't like being struck by lightning, it's like being in a warm, summer rain." I didn't even know what I was saying and there was no planned speech, no rehearsed words or proposal. "Move to Portland. Be with me. Marry me."

A tear slid down her cheek and her lip trembled. Our eyes were locked for an eternity and my emotions quieted. She might not want to be with me now, she might be worried about our communication issues, my past, but she loved me. She wanted to be with me. I was confident of that.

Finally, she broke eye contact and took my phone from me and typed her own note below mine.

*I don't even know who I am.*

"You're who you've always been. Your name, your birth doesn't define you. You're Chloe and Ekaterina. You're the sum total of every day of your twenty-one years of life. And I know who you are. You're sweet and generous and caring, you're thoughtful and funny and sometimes pretty damn sassy. You're you, and you are meant for me."

I had no expectations. I had no desperate need to convince her, no frustration, no anger. It was like in reaching this island, in reaching her, I had finally found a place of peace, contentment, no matter what she said in response.

Chloe took my cheeks between her small hands and stroked

my bottom lip. The way she looked at me- that deep, aching tenderness- made me feel like no man had ever been as loved.

Then she leaned in and spoke so softly if she hadn't been right against my ear I wouldn't have heard her. Then again, maybe I would have.

"I love you," she whispered. "I do."

When we kissed on the front porch of her father's house, it wasn't urgent or anxious or demanding. It was loving, sensual, profound. It was a kiss that spoke volumes and a touch that was more intimate than any other.

We sat there together my arms wrapped around her and after our kisses trailed off, she leaned against me. I just held her and we stared out into the night, to the ocean, the island quiet. The crash of waves was distant, the interior of her house silent except for the murmuring of voices from the TV.

In the silence, we told each other everything.

*For a split second when I realized Anya didn't want to see me and I figured out Ethan had lied to me, I thought about disappearing. I thought about starting with a new identity, one all my own. Created by me. But then I realized that I had already done that. Ethan was right, I was the accumulation of my life, my thoughts, my experiences.*

*My dreams.*

*I never thought that I would meet a guy like Ethan, who could pick whatever girl he wanted, and that he would be content with me. But he was and even when I hesitated, I knew that I wanted to be with him. Forever.*

*Sometimes people talk just to fill the silence.*

*Ethan and I just live.*

*Someday my voice will come back in its entirety, and when it does, Ethan will be there.*

*In Russian I can tell him, "Here is my heart, it is full of love."*

*And he always gives the right response.*

Thanks so much for reading *Meant For Me!* You've just read the fourth story in the Blurred Lines series.
The series order is as follows.

Anya Volkov was adopted from Russia as a child, only to be rejected a year later, deemed 'difficult.' After a lifetime of bouncing from foster home to foster home Anya is living in the East Village and scraping by playing gigs in small clubs, and facing eviction. She'll do whatever it takes to keep a roof over the head of herself and her one year old son. Including making nice with the twin she doesn't remember and stealing baby food from a grocery store.

*Always needed...*

Kane Dermott doesn't want to bust the pierced and sexy woman stealing at the grocery but neither does he want to help her or believe her sob story. Being a cop and the oldest of six siblings with a single mom, he's always the one doing the right thing. The one everyone depends on. The good guy. For once he just wants to have some fun with the hot girl, and Anya is more than willing to make him forget her petty theft in the most delicious way possible.

But it turns out the sob story is real and in the murky world of black market babies, Anya and her son are in danger, and Kane can't walk away from the mysterious and broken woman he has come to love. But neither can he trust her.

*When lies are truth and truths are lies, sometimes only love is the answer...*

Want to know when my next book is out? Sign up for my newsletter e-mail list at
www.erinmccarthy.net/newsletter-2/
follow me on Twitter at @authorerin
or like my Facebook page at
www.facebook.com/ErinMcCarthyBooks.

I appreciate all reviews—they help readers find my books. Please take a moment and leave a review. Thanks!
Check out my other New Adult titles available now:

**TRUE BELIEVERS SERIES**
*True*
*Sweet*
*Believe*
*Shatter*

Made in United States
North Haven, CT
19 May 2022

19323836R00124